THE CUBES MEANT PEACE —
BUT WAS IT
TO BE THE PEACE OF THE GRAVE?

While he was shipwrecked on a distant Jovian moon, with only a cryptic monster for a companion, Paul Shannon had longed for the laughter and friendship of men and women. But when at long last he brought his repaired space craft back to the familiar skies of North America, he was shocked to find AN EARTH GONE MAD.

Men's ambitions, women's love, and the eternal clash of wills, had all given way to the passive docility of stunned beasts. A new cult, born in the stars, was sweeping the world, promising glory but bringing only complete mental submission. And Shannon was torn between unwilling belief and panicky horror as he realized that he himself held the only key to that cosmic riddle.

AN EARTH GONE MAD is a terrific experience in science-fiction adventure!

CAST OF CHARACTERS

PAUL SHANNON

He returned home after a long interplanetary exile to find himself still a stranger on an unearthly Earth!

CARL GARRICK

Because he believed in the Cubes, he faced violent death without lifting a finger.

ZIMMER CONNISTON

This burly labor leader believed that the only way to save humanity was to kill a lot of people.

ELLEN KEYNE

The girl Paul had left behind still loved him, but it was no longer necessary to talk of marriage.

DACE NUGENT

This engineer designed a space-going Ark to weather a mental Flood.

GIL LUCAS

He knew all that science would ever know about the Cubes—yet he knew practically nothing!

THE KYRIL

This featureless beast was content to remain the sole intelligent inhabitant of a lonely moon.

AN EARTH
GONE MAD

by ROGER DEE

CHAPTER ONE

THE KYRIL lay on the flinty Ionian hillside like a domed, lichened boulder, its unfeatured lumpishness denied by the cool certainty of its telepathic voice. "I am a self-sufficient creature, Paul Shannon," it said. "But I think I shall miss you."

The man squatted silently beside it, considering the battered little one-man craft that waited for him at the foot of the slope. In the thin sunlight the ship's name, *Flora*, stood out sharply, and under it, in dwindling sequence: *Solar Services, Inc.*, and a serial made illegible by the scars of an earlier collision.

Below the ship sprawled an obsidian nightmare of badlands, glass-bright and jagged, and beyond swayed a sullen jungle of flame-vines and barbed underbrush where the lava-lions hunted.

The man stood up restlessly on bare, calloused feet. His hair hung to his shoulders, longer and blacker than the tangle of beard that swept his chest; he wore nothing but a brief clout of animal hide, and exposure had browned his skin even on a world so far from its parent sun.

"I'm an engineer, not a mechanic nor an astrogator," he said. "I'd never have repaired the *Flora* and laid a course without your help, Kyril, not in two years nor in a hundred. But now—"

"Now you are ready to go," the Kyril agreed. "You have learned a great deal here, Paul Shannon, but you have changed more than you know. You may wish, later, that you had remained here."

The man shook his head. "You're wrong, for once. It's been hell here, what with the lava-lions hunting me and

5

knowing that Ellen has been waiting for me for two years. She and Gil Lucas—the world may have forgotten me, but never those two."

He touched the Kyril's gray-green shell affectionately. "You hid yourself from men before I came. I won't give you away."

He felt the Kyril's shrug, an enigmatic pulse of no-thought. "When you reach Earth," it said, "I shall have no need of secrecy."

The man stared, his gray eyes puzzled. "I wish I knew more about you. Sometimes I think you're more than you admit, a great deal more. Can you see into the future, Kyril?"

When there was no answer he knew that the Kyril, after its fashion, had withdrawn itself. The *Flora* waited in deepening shadow below, its presence fanning the man's eagerness to be gone. The Sun, coin-sized and golden, sank behind a jagged horizon; with its going, the vast flattened dome of Jupiter rose, banded and glowing.

Shannon shivered against the growing chill. "I'm going to miss you, too," he said. "Goodbye, Kyril. . . ."

He came down too fast, knowing the risk but afraid to demand too much of his jury-rigged deceleration gear. Half his mind was spring-tense with the strain of gauging speed and distance without proper instruments; the other half considered hungrily the long crescent sweep of Earth rising to meet him, her day side a mottled mosaic of greens and browns and water-glints, her night side vague and mysterious under its moon-bright mantle of clouds.

He did not try to choose a landing site. It was enough to be back, to see that great soft curve flattening and reversing under him, rising to receive him like a vast convex cradle. *Home.*

It did not matter where he put down. He was a responsible agent of the most powerful financial enterprise in history; the comet-and-crescent emblem of Solar Services assured him of respect and assistance anywhere, and once he reached a radophone   .

Still the rosy glow of a city's lights against the night heartened him. He would land in a civilized place, where he could orient himself and shed his barbarous beard and mane of hair before he called Ellen Keyne and Gil Lucas.

The city-glow swerved away. Small points of light crept, snail-like, to and from it along a web of far, serpentine paths: surface cars, speed slowed to a crawl by distance. A single isolated light speared upward, a dark building loomed squarely in the curve of his landing arc—

He struck with a thunderous crash that left him half stunned, fighting for breath. Violet flame from the *Flora's* landing jets flared outward, searing the earth until he found the valve and shut off the flow of fuel. He fumbled for the port control, drew it down and let in a cool night wind heavy with the smell of charred grass and damp soil.

A door opened in the building ahead, spilling a crooked rectangle of yellow lamplight across the night, and he saw that it was a farmhouse and that a white ribbon of highway lay between the ship and the light. A man came out of the house, bare-headed and shirt-sleeved, bulking huge in silhouette. A woman's voice drifted after him, bell-clear and unexcited: "Hurry, Carl. Someone may be hurt."

The man crossed highway and smoking turf to stand in the ship's open port. The *Flora's* panel lights illuminated him palely, a massive young man with curling light hair and blue eyes. He was smiling as from long habit, his face calm and unsurprised, his whole bearing charged with contentment and another quality harder to define.

"Are you hurt, friend?" he asked, and came into the ship. His big hands touched Shannon gently. "We had expected someone else. . . . Let me help you into our house."

They crossed the roadway together, Shannon leaning on the big man's arm and shivering in the night-wind. In a

7

neat, bare living room a young woman met them, belting on a coarse gray robe over her nightgown. She smiled at Shannon without speaking, her face no more dismayed by his wild look than the man's had been. She was small and slender and red-haired, and the same quality that had puzzled Shannon in the big man's bearing was repeated in her eyes like an echo: a great calmness, and a peace beyond the definition of peace.

"I am Carl Garrick," the man said. "My wife, Olive. We are farmers and Cubists."

"You are at home in our home," the woman said.

For a moment the eyes of the couple caught and held, and when they smiled together it came to Shannon with an unexpected shock of surprise that their strangeness stemmed from possession of a quality he had never truly met with before: serenity.

They seated him at a rough table, and the man brought a blanket which Shannon draped about himself gratefully. The woman disappeared into the kitchen and returned with a glass of warm milk.

"We can't give you coffee," she said. "We never go into the city; it upsets the Normals, and they are troubled enough already."

Shannon stared at the glass, fascinated by the tiny ripples that danced over its creamy white liquid from the movement of her hands. His throat constricted in a sudden agony of anticipation.

"My God, milk!" he said. "I'd forgotten it existed."

"I'll make supper for you," the woman said. She looked toward the kitchen. "Carl!"

Carl Garrick came out with a steaming bowl of water, scissors and an ancient folding razor. "The hermit life makes for independence," he said. "We've even learned to trim each other's hair. May I try my hand on yours while my wife cooks?"

Wonder grew in Shannon, and shame touched him for

the first time when he realized how unkempt and desperate he must look.

"You are kind," he said. "In the cities, no one would bother."

He thought of Ellen then and his old urgency brought him up short, fretting at even this delay. "Do you have a radophone here?"

Garrock shook his head. "No. There is no one to call."

"No one? But I saw the city lights!"

They laughed together. "That would have been Denver," Garrick said. "Or Brighton, though Denver's skyglow would be greater. I meant that there is no one whom *we* might call except the Servants, who would come for us if they needed us. There are no radophones in the Sanctuaries."

To Shannon it was like a foreign language, clear of sound but meaning nothing. It left him baffled and vaguely uneasy.

"I don't understand. I've been—away—for two years, and I'm out of touch. Why can't you call anyone, or go into town?"

An earlier reference returned to fan his disquiet. "What are Cubists and Normals and Servants and Sanctuaries?"

They stared at him blankly. "But everyone—" Olive began. She turned to her husband, her eyes wide. "Garrick, he *doesn't* know about the Cubes!"

"Then I'll tell him about them," Garrick said with unshaken serenity, "while I trim his hair, and while you make supper."

For the first time in two years Shannon was fed to fullness. Garrick's coarse gray clothing hung slackly on his slighter frame; he was washed and shaved, his hair cut short by Garrick's surprisingly expert hands. Olive brought him a mirror and he stared, appalled, at the change in himself.

He had lost twenty pounds. The hair at his temples was touched with gray, and the thin, hard face that stared back at him was like a stranger's. He was not the same man who had left Earth and Ellen two years ago.

Thought of Ellen stirred him and made him conscious of Carl Garrick's voice, finishing its monologue: "—people called them *star dice* at first, because they were square like dies and because they came to us from space. But all that is changed now. They are the Cubes.

"No one knows where they really came from, nor how their Change is brought about. The Servants who trained us at Ohio Peace Center after we left the Toledo Sanctuary, taught us that such questions have no meaning—the great truth is that the Cubes are here, waking men from their unreason and bringing peace. They solve every problem and lift every burden."

Shannon, drowsing under the measured snicking of scissors and the murmur of Garrick's voice, had not caught more than an occasional word. He had not really cared; manias came and went in an unsettled world where unrest and dissension pyramided with every generation, and his first interest had given way quickly to a half-waking anticipation of tomorrow.

He put down the mirror when Garrick finished. "It's a new cult, then. A religion."

"Not a cult," Carl said. He and Olive looked at each other, smiling. "Nor a religion. It's *reality*, the perfection men would have learned ages ago if they hadn't taken the wrong turning."

"Reality? What sort of reality?"

"You can't possibly understand until you visit a Cube and go through the change yourself," Carl said. "Could you describe a sunset to a man born blind, or a symphony to one born deaf?"

For the first time since his crash on Io, Shannon laughed. "If visiting a Cube will make me as happy as you two, I'll see one the minute I get back to Boston Suburban. God knows I need a change of disposition, after these past two years!"

An Earth Gone Mad

"The Cubes help all who come to them," Olive said. Her hand found Carl's and clung. "Carl was a muscler for Solar Services in Toledo before our Change, and we never knew what peace and security were. It was rough and dangerous work and he hated it, but Solar wouldn't release him for a Guild job—the syndicates pay their musclers to suppress unrest among employees, you know, and the Guild fights back with its own squads. ."

This much at least was familiar. Shannon had seen the ancient tug-of-war played out between Guild and syndicate more times than he cared to remember, and neither, no matter how any single contest ended, had ever seemed to gain any permanent advantage.

"There was a riot that brought me to my senses," Carl said. "I killed a Guild worker and had to run for it until Solar cleared me with Government—but by then the Guild had marked me down on its retaliation list, and I knew I'd never run far enough to escape them. So I went to a Sanctuary for help, and Olive went with me. The Servants of the Cubes took us to Ohio Peace Center for training, and when we were ready they sent us here."

"And nothing," Olive finished, "can ever take our happiness from us now. Guild retaliation doesn't frighten us, nor the danger of the Normals rising against us. Our part of the Plan is to set peace before the world as a reality instead of as an abstract, and we are doing it."

Shannon's wandering glance found the old-fashioned calendar clock on the mantelpiece, and restlessness stirred him again when he made out the reading: *June 17, 2319, 0400.*

"How far is it to Brighton?" he asked. "I've got to get to a radophone and—" He caught himself up when they smiled at each other. "You're right. After two years, another night shouldn't matter."

They nodded together, shoulders touching, something in the serene unity between them proclaiming a welding of affection beyond Shannon's understanding.

11

"I think you'd like to tell us about those two years," Olive said. "I know we'd like to hear."

And he found himself talking, his hardly acquired caution melting before their eager interest, and in the telling he felt a slow sublimation of the bitterness that had driven him for so long.

"I was on my way to Callisto to make a construction estimate when it happened," he said. "It was an important assignment, a special project of Solar Service President Orsham's, and it meant a great deal to me. To Ellen, too, because we were to be married as soon as the estimate was finished.

"But I never reached Callisto. The propulsion pile of my ship went wrong somehow, and I crashed on Io instead."

He was amazed to discover how distant it all seemed now. "I wouldn't have lived a day but for the Kyril," he said. "He seemed to know everything; he spotted food for me and woke me when the lava-lions prowled too near. I learned to sleep in his shadow. I used to tell him about Ellen and the plans we made and the evenings we spent together, sometimes just the two of us, sometimes with Gil Lucas. Gil is my best friend, a mathematician and physicist, heading his own little research enterprise. . .   Ellen lives with her parents in Boston Suburban, and I had a small apartment in Boston Metro near the Solar offices. It was a good life."

He frowned, considering an old and puzzling problem. "No one ever found intelligent life in the solar system before I crashed on Io. There's a small tribe of native yellow pygmies on Titan, but they're subhuman and are under Government protection. . .   I had an idea that the Kyril was not a solarian at all, but he would never tell me. He taught me a great deal, though, and helped me to—"

He broke off at a sound outside. "What's that?"

The three of them went to the door together, Carl and Olive Garrick holding hands like children. The white glare of a surface car's sodium lamps blinded them briefly, swinging off the highway into the farmyard.

"Normals," Carl said, his voice untroubled. "And perhaps the Guild retaliation we were expecting when your ship landed. It doesn't matter that they've found us. The Plan will be served."

His wife repeated the words like an echo. "The Plan will be served."

CHAPTER TWO

THE LIGHTS blinked off outside.

Four dark figures piled out of the car and converged swiftly upon the house. When they entered the rectangle of light from the open doorway Shannon felt the set purpose behind their approach, and sudden premonition set the hair to prickling along his neck.

They paused briefly at the steps. Shannon, with mounting uneasiness, saw that two of them were armed not with the familiar quartz-lensed shock-rods of civil police but with flat, lethal dart-guns.

"Watch the exits," a voice said heavily. "Fulmer goes with me."

They scattered. "They won't run," someone said, protestingly. "Cubies never do."

The two armed men came inside, not alike in face or build but wearing upon them a singleness of purpose that woke Shannon's old wariness instantly to life.

These men he could understand. They *hated.*

He backed away, his glance searching the room for a weapon and finding none. The two men ignored the Garricks to watch him, narrow-eyed. The leader made a suggestive movement with his gun.

"You're no Cubie," he said. "What are you doing here?"

Carl Garrick answered for Shannon. "He is a stranger

13

who needed help, not one of us. Let him go."

They ignored him, and he fell silent. Olive moved closer to him, catching his hand again, and they smiled at each other with a serenity that utterly disregarded danger.

"You should have known better than ask help of a Cubie," the leader said to Shannon. "It's a mistake you won't make twice."

"Wait," Shannon said. His voice was thin even to his own ears. "What are you going to do?"

They laughed like jackals baying together. "The Cubie treatment," Fulmer said. "You're going to Cubie heaven, where the star dice roll. What did you expect?"

Garrick touched Shannon's arm. "We expected this. It comes to many of us even in the cities. But we'll be replaced many times over, and that's all that matters."

Shannon stared at him in disbelief. "You knew you'd be murdered here sooner or later? You're not going to resist now?"

"Not all of these men will have been on such an errand before," Carl said. His smile was as free as ever. "What they do tonight will so burden them that in the end at least one will go to a Sanctuary to be at peace with himself. What happens here will happen over and over until some day every human being on Earth will have made the Change, and then there will be peace. Forever."

The truth, overlooked before, left Shannon stunned. This was more than another stupid utopian cult; it was a thing stronger and more dangerous than armed revolution. And these men with guns were the inevitable retaliation, a force crying the Normal resentment, coming in darkness to snuff by violence a flame not lighted by hands.

"That's enough," the leader said. He took a little metal cylinder from a pocket and tossed it toward the back of the room. "Let's get it over with."

The incendiary was still in the air when Shannon lunged. Fulmer, his eyes on the arcing bomb, was caught off guard;

14

Shannon's shoulder took him in the chest and drove him headlong through the doorway and out into the night. The soft *phut* of the leader's dart-gun followed them. Flame tore the porch steps behind them as they plunged downward.

They struck heavily, Fulmer underneath, Shannon clutching blindly for the weapon.

One of the men guarding the exits came out of the darkness and struck viciously at Shannon's head with a club. He threw himself aside somehow and the blow caught him instead on the shoulder. Agony tore him, and with the pain came a red, destroying anger.

He knelt upon the winded Fulmer and wrenched the dart-gun from his hand. Two years before, the lethal feel of the weapon would have sickened him; now it snuggled comfortingly into his hand, urging him on with its cold metal will to be used.

He blasted the man with the club first, at arm's reach. A second figure ran toward him out of the night, and he cut it down as coldly as he would have potted a target in a shooting gallery.

He ran for the house then, knowing already that he was too late when the muffled thumping of another dart-gun sounded inside. A gust of bitter white smoke met him at the door; through it he saw Carl and Olive Garrick tumbled together in a motionless, broken heap.

The leader burst through the smoke, flame still licking at his heels. Shannon shot him down and ran back into the night, still raging. There was another. Fulmer, from whom he had taken the gun—

The man was gone.

The surface car loomed up in the darkness, metal curves highlighted redly in the fire-glow. Shannon hauled himself into it and swerved it, turbomotor screaming, onto the highway. Its sodium lights, when he snapped them on, outlined starkly the running figure of Fulmer, plunging desperately to get off the pavement.

15

Shannon ran him down as carefully as he would have crushed a spider under his heel.

Afterward, he let the machine out and rocketed through the night with anger dying in him and nausea clogging his throat. The sky-glow of Brighton rose before him at once and he slowed his speed, trying to find some thread of reason in the nightmare that had caught him up.

He had come home to violence and hatred and a fanaticism beyond idiocy—and to what else? If an atrocity like this could happen in a once-quiet countryside, then what might have come over the rest of the world?

Could it be like this everywhere?

The thought of Ellen Keyne was like a breath of sanity out of madness. He had to get to her, or to Gil Lucas, and learn from someone he could trust what had happened to the world.

He pressed the accelerator and the lights of Brighton swept nearer, resolving into a checkered pattern of street lamps and windows already paling under the first pink glow of sunrise.

At the edge of town he met other cars, headlamps glaring. Later he saw knots of early risers on street corners, yawning and shuffling, waiting for local turbobuses. Not one of them wore the sort of rough gray clothing that Carl Garrick had given to Shannon, and he reasoned that it was a garb peculiar to Cubists; he would have to get rid of it quickly, before the hunt overtook him.

For there must be a hunt. Even in a countryside so unsettled, the burning farmhouse with its dead would bring investigation, and he was a stranger in Cubist clothing and a stolen machine.

He remembered the *Flora* then and felt the net close tighter about him. The police would check her identity with Solar Services and from that instant would be after him in earnest, armed with descriptions and photographs.

He suffered a moment of utter panic at the prospect. To

16

be hunted endlessly, like an animal, through a strange country

The craggy desolation of Io flashed before him like a lost haven, and he recalled the Kyril's telepathic warning: *You may wish, later, that you had remained here.*

He shook off the mood and slowed the car while he searched for a practical escape from his dilemma. There was no question of going to the local authorities; his only safe alternative was to get back to Boston Metro and Solar Services, whose influence would protect him. Among friends, with Ellen and Gil Lucas behind him, he would be infinitely more able to defend himself against any charges made.

A passenger shuttle flared up from a port somewhere across the town, and the sight made him stop the car in sudden speculation. The shuttle was gone at once, but high above it in the red wash of sunrise he saw the pale violet arc of a stratoliner dropping down to Denver.

It might as well have been halfway across the continent.

To reach Boston Metro he would have to board that liner, and he had no money. He could not even be sure that one in Cubist clothing would be allowed passage. He might be arrested or mobbed; at best he would be remembered, and the chase would close tighter.

It might be safer to call for help than to run. There would be a Solar office in Denver, and once he reported his difficulty the syndicate could not refuse him help.

He left the car and stood briefly in the waning light of a street lamp, looking up and down the silent street for the jagged fluorescent thunderbolt emblem that would mark the local radophone exchange. He found none, but sight of a lighted restaurant across the street promised a coin-station instrument inside. With luck—

The restaurant was warm and bright when he entered, the air heavy with the smell of frying bacon and coffee in the making. At so early an hour it was all but deserted: behind the counter a fat cook scrambled eggs with a busy

17

sizzling of grease; three men on counter stools ate with one eye on their newspapers; a fourth customer waited for his order, fingers drumming impatiently on the bar.

The unoccupied man saw Shannon first. He stood up, anger and something like fear altering the bored cast of his face.

"Cubie!" he said. "What the hell?"

The three at the counter looked up sharply, faces reflecting identical degrees of astonishment. The cook shut off the gas under his grill and came toward Shannon, his fat face angry.

"We don't serve Cubies here," he said. "Get out!"

Their common antagonism was like a physical force, thrusting him away. Necessity made Shannon stiffen himself against it and force down his resentment.

"I'm not a Cubist," he said. "I've been in—an accident. There's no time to explain, but if you'll let me use your radophone—"

The customers looked at each other in silent agreement. The fat cook put a hand under his counter and brought out a patrolman's truncheon, a wicked foot-long tube of leaded rubber and spring steel.

"You've got a nerve," he said. "Coming in here like a human being. . . . This is a Guild-manned restaurant, didn't you see our sign? Get out or I'll break your head for you!"

The five of them moved toward Shannon, grouping together. Shannon felt the door against his back and went out hastily, leaving them staring after him and talking angrily among themselves. It was not until the door swung shut after him that he remembered the dart-gun in his jacket pocket; recalling it brought a momentary impulse to go inside again and demand a hearing, but he put the thought from him. He had trouble enough already.

A moment later, turning his stolen car at the next corner, he found that the incident had been unnecessary from the beginning.

18

An Earth Gone Mad

The local radophone center lay just ahead, a small white building brilliantly advertised by the familiar blue thunderbolt flashing across its facade. He left the car at the curb before it and went in warily, a hand on the weapon in his jacket pocket.

The exchange was empty except for a clerk, thin and young and sallow, who drowsed at the change window. Shannon went toward him softly, looming over the grill before the gaping attendant realized that he was not alone.

"I must make a call at once," Shannon said. He watched the startled clerk narrowly, anticipating the same reaction he had met with at the restaurant. "I have no money, but can establish credit. If you'll let me—"

"You're no Cubie," the clerk said. He stood up, anxiety edging his voice. "More likely an intelligence agent, Government or syndicate—" He broke off sharply. "Are the Guilds rising?"

He began to sweat when Shannon did not answer. "I'm not a Guild operator, I'm a Communications Independent. If the Guild demonstrates here, my life won't be worth a bogus credit!"

"I'm not an agent," Shannon said. "I—"

The clerk went white. "Then you're a Guild spy, passing yourself as a Cubie. I might have known it!"

Without warning he plunged a hand under the change counter and brought up a shock-rod. Shannon snatched at it instinctively; his fingers closed on the quartz-lensed head, reversing it in the other's hand.

The rod glowed briefly, already activated by the clerk's touch. Its pale blue beam caught the man in the chest and sent him sliding limply from sight behind his wicket.

Without a glance at the unconscious clerk Shannon caught up a handful of coins and turned back to the radophone booths. The fellow would be out for perhaps half an hour; there would be time to make his call, but little enough for explanations.

19

An Earth Gone Mad

In the nearest booth Shannon hesitated, sweating with the effort of deciding what call to make first. Solar Services, once he had established his identity, would certainly come to his aid—but he knew the endless delay and verification that must follow the call, the relaying of request through overlapping channels of authority. The clerk might rouse first, or some early patron surprise him. The men at the restaurant might already have notified the local patrol.   .

He could not risk calling Solar now. It must be either Ellen Keyne or Gil Lucas, trusting that one of them could reach high enough into Solar circles to send help quickly.

Much as he longed to see her, the requirement eliminated Ellen automatically. He must get through to Gil.

He closed the booth door, his hands busy with the selector bank before the hush of privacy had fallen. The muted hum of open circuit died. The radophone screen lighted with bold, stiff words: *BOSTON MET INF.*

"Lucas, Gilbert F.," Shannon said into the microphone orifice.

The screen flickered. *Lucas, Gilbert F. Physicist. Residence 1220 Antoine. Code. AN67944.*

Shannon shifted in his caller's seat, sweating again with tension. To be so close, with so little time . . .

"Announce Paul Shannon," he said. "Brighton, Colorado. Ring at once, receiver's charge."

Robot controls juggled distant relays. Shannon waited, wiping damp palms against the rough fabric of his jacket.

The man who appeared on the screen was small and fat and middle-aged, with sparse gray hair carefully brushed to cover a bald spot. His intent small eyes held no slightest trace of sleep.

"I don't know you," the man said. "What do you want?"

"I am calling Gilbert Lucas," Shannon said. "I'm a very old friend of his. Will you put him on the circuit, please?"

The fat man considered him dispassionately. "Radophone Control is getting lax," he said. "This number should have been cleared long ago. No one named Lucas has lived in this apartment for at least thirteen months."

The screen flickered and went blank.

Frustration made Shannon almost ill. There was no time to demand a manual check of Boston Metro radophone files; the clerk might wake at any moment, the police might be closer than he had thought. .

The feel of the dart-gun in his pocket decided him.

The car outside might get him out of Brighton, and once in Denver he could apply in person to Solar Services. Failing there, he still had the melodramatic—but direct—alternative of forcing his way aboard an eastbound stratoliner at Denver Port.

CHAPTER THREE

ESCAPING BRIGHTON, when he came to it, was easier than he had expected.

At such an early hour another speeding car attracted no attention; he reached Denver, a few minutes later, without having once been challenged. It was not until he had entered the city proper and had picked out the towering comet-and-crescent spire of Denver's Solar Services building that his Cubist clothing first drew stares.

Occasionally now he saw gray-clad Cubists on the streets, smiling and unhurried, unmolested here where the machinery of the law functioned more normally. But none drove cars, and he guessed that it was contrary to custom for Cubists to operate private machines. Wary of attention, he left the car on the first stretch of empty street and went ahead on foot.

He had not far to go.

A few blocks ahead a stratoliner roared up, chemical takeoff jets screaming, and when he rounded the final corner he found himself at the steel-mesh fence that encircled the Denver stratoport. At the opposite end of the field and behind the port's latticed signal tower rose the commanding bulk of the Solar Services building.

He went toward it briskly past shops just opening for the day's business, trying now that he was afoot to meet the stares of passersby with something of a Cubist's expected serenity.

But near the entrance ramp he paused, struck by a sudden dissatisfaction with the imposing facade before him. He had looked forward to this moment of return second only to his reunion with Ellen and Gil. But now the power of Solar Services, exemplified by the massive arrogance of her western headquarters, irritated him obscurely. Before his exile on Io his standing with the syndicate had been a matter of personal pride, lending a sense of being not a cog in an impersonal machine but an individual member of a respected—and, so far as was practical—indulgent family.

But it came to him now with something of a shock that once he had found Ellen and Gil and had claimed the two years of accumulated salary waiting for him he must inevitably go back to making routine construction estimates for Solar, and the thought depressed him. Until now he had taken that resumption of duty for granted, not dreaming that he should feel this sudden premonitory stir of restlessness.

Could he go back to his old grind after having known the calm logic of the Kyril and the blood-hunger of the lava-lions? The demands of survival on Io had forced upon him a capacity for instant decision and swift competence of action; could he be happy again at compiling dull data for the building of import warehouses and satellite exchange depots?

He was not permitted to find out.

At the ramp, a small enclosed van drew up to the curb and stopped beside him, turbomotor idling. A man, quietly dressed and unremarkable, stepped out to bar his way.

"We had expected you earlier, Mr. Shannon," the man said. "Will you get inside, Mr. Shannon? There isn't much time left."

Dismay chilled Shannon like a plunge into icy water. "Civil police?" he asked. "You move fast!"

The man said patiently, "We're not police. Get into the van."

22

An Earth Gone Mad

Shannon turned, estimating his chances. The van driver held a shock-rod ready, its conical lens resting on the lowered side-glass in line with Shannon's chest. Shannon stepped into the van, moving toward the rear at the driver's gesture. The vehicle was empty except for a suspension rack that held a freshly pressed suit of casual brown tweeds and a neat array of accessory garments: white shirt, tie, underclothing and street shoes.

The man on the street came in and closed the door. "We've no time for questions, Mr. Shannon. Please put on the clothing."

He frowned faintly when Shannon did not move. "Don't force us to shock you and dress you. This is more important than you know."

Shannon stripped off his rough gray Cubist garments and slipped into the tweeds. They hung on him loosely but he found himself, without thought, approving the cut and material. He had owned a similar suit once, before his unlucky Callistan mission—Ellen had helped him select it, matching color and style to blend with his dark skin and black hair.

He patted the pockets automatically, and felt the unmistakable outline of a wallet in his jacket pocket.

"I don't understand any of this," he said. He was being handled like an unruly child, and the thought angered him. "Will you drop your telemovie dramatics and tell me what you want?"

"You'll know in good time," the driver said.

He put away his shock-rod and touched a panel stud. The van purred into motion, made a right turn and leaned into an ascending curve. There was presently the sensation of climbing a gently sloping ramp; the van stopped and the driver stepped out. Shannon, following, found himself inside the steel fence of the stratoplane port, a short stone's throw from the flight terminal.

"You'll find money and a ticket to Boston Metro in the wallet," the man said. "You have four minutes to make the stratoliner at Ramp Seven."

When Shannon stared at him blankly, he said patiently, "Don't delay. You'll know more when you're ready for it."

The van slid away.

23

An Earth Gone Mad

Shannon, more bewildered than ever, went into the terminal to find Ramp Seven. The brown leather wallet in his pocket yielded a thin sheaf of yellow credit notes, and a single-passage ticket which the flight attendant accepted without remark. A trim stewardess in buff Solar uniform showed him to his seat.

He settled himself beside a port with a sense of unreality that all but made him pinch himself. An hour earlier he had been a fugitive in flight, straining every faculty to escape a tightening net of disaster. Now, without choice, he was on his way to Boston Metro, his problem solved.

By whom, and why?

The improbability of it startled him with a sudden suspicion of his sanity. Was he really here on a stratoliner, bound for Metro? Had he actually landed a jury-rigged *Flora* outside Brighton and raged through that nightmare of violence at the Garricks'?

Or was he wandering senselessly across the glassy badlands of Io, his mind snapped at last under the strain of survival?

A man sat down beside him, and Shannon, turning, found the face real beyond any imagining: spectacled, jowled, smoothly substantial, it could be no possible part of madness.

"Look," the passenger said. His glance directed Shannon's through the port to another liner loading in the adjacent cradle. "My God, how long will it be till we're all like that?"

At the other liner a solid gray line of men and women in Cubist garb filed up to the loading ramp, moving with unhurried, termitic deliberation. Shannon could make out their faces plainly; they smiled without exception, radiating the same serenity he had sensed in the Garricks.

"They're bound for Ohio Peace Center," the passenger said. "The third shipment this week, and the training consignments get bigger every time. Where will it end, I ask?"

They looked at each other wonderingly, and in the man's eyes Shannon caught a hint of the same puzzled terror he had seen in the men who had forced him out of the restaurant in Brighton.

24

An Earth Gone Mad

"I've no idea," Shannon said.

Then, caution prompting him to hide his ignorance: "I'm afraid I'm out of touch. I've been on Outer Planet duty for two years, Neptune sector, and all we get there is rumor."

The man eyed him curiously. "I thought so. You've got the look of a spaceman or a colonist. You'll find things changed."

The rising of his own liner saved Shannon further conversation for the moment. He settled back in his seat, forgetting the man beside him, and watched the stratoport buildings dwindle from sight below. Moments later the atomic propulsors came on, driving the ship through the last of atmosphere and into a paradox of indigo night that held both Sun and stars.

For the first time Shannon relaxed, putting the puzzle of his deliverance away from him. All facts but one became unimportant; in two hours more he would be in Boston Metro and on his way to Ellen.

In the quiet of airless flight, the man beside Shannon moved restlessly. "I've wondered," he said, "if Solar Services is using Cubists on the outer planets. They're using them here, you know."

The knowledge jolted Shannon roughly out of his haze of anticipation. "As personnel? I shouldn't think them capable."

"Then they haven't spread that far," the man said. His eyes blinked musingly behind their spectacles. "But they will. In time, they'll reach everywhere."

"I'm sorry," Shannon said, and stood up abruptly. "But I'm not familiar enough with conditions to discuss them. I'll learn soon enough, I suppose."

He went back to the lavatory, sizing up the other passengers as he went and wondering if he might not be still under surveillance. A soft lot, he thought, largely businessmen and tourists wealthy enough to afford stratoliner passage; not one of them had the force of purpose he had felt in the men who had put him aboard the liner.

With the lavatory door bolted, he took out the wallet and examined it carefully.

It contained two hundred credits, enough under normal circumstances to last for perhaps a week. The amount, he thought, might have some significance—if further manipulation of his affairs were intended, it would come within a week's time.

The wallet contained identification papers as well as money. He drew them out of their glassite case and scanned them with an astonishment that grew to incredulity.

They were stamped with a date two years old and placed him unequivocally as Paul Shannon, construction engineer for Solar Services, Inc. There was an unmistakably genuine full-face photograph of himself, and a black indelible whorl of his index fingers.

It was his own wallet.

For a long time after replacing it in his pocket he stood without moving, staring at his reflection in the lavatory mirror and trying to fit this new improbability into the tangle of contradictions that meshed him in. He remembered the wallet well, an old one he had left behind when he set out for Callisto—

Left in his Boston Metro apartment, in the pockets of a brown tweed suit.

He knew even before he took off the suit jacket and looked at the tailor's label what he would find, but the proof startled him in spite of his conviction. Neatly stitched, stylized letters spelled out in red thread his own name: *Paul T. Shannon.*

His apartment would long ago have been let to someone else, but his clothing and wallet had been removed. By whom, and why?

He gave up wondering finally, conceding defeat until he had more information. He went back to the passenger section, choosing an empty seat for privacy, and tried to sit without thinking while the stars marched past outside the port.

The blonde stewardess paused beside him on her way forward and gave him a more than professional smile, her eyes openly interested.

"I don't remember you from previous trips," she said brightly. "Is there anything I can get for you, sir?"

He watched the movement of her discreetly painted mouth, matching the sound of her voice against his memory of other women's voices, against Ellen Keyne's. He had for-gotten more than he realized, on Io.

And suddenly the lost years were no more than a van-ished, improbable dream, a dissolving figment of nightmare. The reassuring sanity of normal living rested upon him like a comforting hand.

"Yes," he said, and felt saliva start at memory of a long-forgotten taste. "Can you get me some cigarettes?"

She smiled again, but her eyes were disappointed. "We don't stock them, but I've some extras in my locker. I'll get them."

She was back almost at once, shaking her head when he felt for his wallet. "Call it a souvenir of the trip, please. I know what it's like to be caught without smokes."

He juggled the bright little carton absently, wanting des-perately to talk to her, to restore through her obvious inter-est in him a quality he had lost without knowing it—assur-ance.

She took the burden of decision from him. "You're on leave?"

"And reassignment," he said. He moved over to the port, making room. "Can you sit with me and talk? I've been off Earth for two years, and there's a great deal I'll have to re-learn."

She made a small sound of surprise. "I'm afraid you're in for a shock, then. Probably an unpleasant one." She looked toward the control cabin. "I can't stay now—I'm needed up front."

Her eyes, when she turned back, were frankly inviting. "But I have a twenty-hour leave in Boston Metro . . ."

Shannon flushed uncomfortably. "I won't be free, in Metro. I've a fiancee who has waited two years there."

She laughed lightly, but her eyes pitied him. "You would. I only hope you find things as you left them. Few do."

She turned to go forward, and hesitated.

"Advice to the innocent," she said. "You won't like the way things are now, but you can't change them back. No one can. There's going to be trouble between the Guild and the syndicates, with the Cubists in the middle. Stay out of it. Go back to space if you have to, but don't be caught in this thing."

Shannon watched her move down the aisle toward the control room, puzzled by her unexpected interest until understanding came.

"I'll be damned," he thought, remembering the hard, wary face that had looked back at him from the lavatory mirror and comparing it with the sleek grooming of the other passengers. "She's mistaken me for an Explorations man or Frontier Guard or something else as glamorous. I must stand out in this crowd like a circus bear!"

The incident set him to thinking about himself, a pastime foreign to his nature, and he considered again the change made in him by the two lost years. He felt a recurrence of the unexpected restlessness that had touched him at the Solar Services ramp in Denver, and with a fresh doubt that he could ever conform again.

He felt the pack of cigarettes in his hand then and ripped it open, shook out a cylinder and puffed it alight. The smoke was rich and smooth in his throat, relaxing the tension that had ridden him. He settled more comfortably into his seat and let his mind run over again the bewildering chain of improbabilities that had brought him here.

And with his relaxing came the only possible solution, an answer stemming from his abortive radophone call in Brighton.

"Gil Lucas!" he said aloud, so sharply that the man ahead started and looked curiously over his shoulder.

The exchange robotics would have announced his name, yet the fat man who had answered had accepted receiver's charges—and then had denied knowing either Shannon or Gil. Why?

Because the fat man was a part of the puzzle. Because he had wanted to make certain that it was Paul Shannon who called.

The fat man must have relayed his call to Gil, for how else could the men with the van have known where to intercept him? No one but Gil could have sent them, or have known where to find his clothing and the wallet with his identification.

28

He found the obvious flaw in his reasoning, and the puzzle fell again into a hopeless confusion of inconsistencies. The suit and wallet must have been waiting for him in Denver, since not even a stratoplane could have brought them there in the short time elapsed between his call and his detention at the Solar ramp. The postulation presupposed that Gil, or someone, had known that he would be in Denver this morning.

And Gil could not have known. No one could.

The knowledge implied in turn that someone had known that Shannon would set down the *Flora* at the Garrick farmhouse in the dark hours of morning, and that his movements had been paced from that moment.

More. It would mean that someone had known where he had spent the past two years. The inference that followed—it was impossible.

He gave it up finally and lit another cigarette, trying to drive the whole contradictory jumble out of his mind. Once he had found Gil Lucas, he could get his explanations at first hand. But tracing Gil through the confusion of Boston Metro would take time, and before he undertook that search a need vastly more important demanded his attention.

He had to get back to Ellen.

CHAPTER FOUR

THE FAMILIAR feverish bustle of Boston Port did nothing to lessen his impatience, but it gave him a measure of reassurance against the sense of unreality that had plagued him. He went rapidly through the busy hive of the terminal, gathering confidence from the well remembered bedlam of motorized baggage carts and the varicolored flashings of schedule boards and pervading hum of voices.

At the outbound gates he let himself be carried along by the press of commuters to a wide, sheltered platform. A local shuttle had just landed and was disgorging passengers into the terminal; it would be empty in a moment, and ready to take him to Boston Suburban.

Close behind him a visinews machine crackled, the commentator's voice reaching with practiced inflection for the passerby's attention. Listeners milled aimlessly about it, jostling Shannon with the commuter's impersonal rudeness. Disjointed fragments of informative gabble filtered through the press:

> .   *Guild head Zimmer Conniston last night delivered an ultimatum to Government Council, threatening wholesale industrial shutdown unless growing employment of Cubists by syndicates is halted.*
> .   *troops rushed to guard Cubist Peace Center in Ohio against possible attack   crisis .   . protective surveillance by civil patrols over local Sanctuaries*
> *Grover Orsham, President of Solar Services, announces counter program to end industrial discrimination against Cubist workers, citing excellent efficiency records set as syndicate employees*

Shannon heard little of it and understood less, but his inevitable conclusion was that the Cubes presented a far more important issue than he had suspected. The Cubist Change was affecting the country's basic economic structure; the talk of Government troops had an ominous sound.

Shannon drifted aboard the emptied shuttle with the crowd, putting his uneasy conjectures out of mind. There would be time enough for them later, after he had seen Ellen.

The shuttle rose and flashed across the terminal yards and the city. Boston Port fell away, and with its going Shannon expelled a ragged breath of relief. He had come four hundred million miles for this, and he had waited two interminable years. He fought impatience now, telling himself that he could wait a few minutes more.

Still he half expected to be met at Boston Suburban by a civil patrol and snatched from his moment of triumph, but the fear was groundless. He was only another passenger alighting from a shuttle, another commuting nonentity lost in the anonymous bustle.

He went through the milling throng to the nearest exit, eyes searching the street beyond for a waiting surface cab.

An Earth Gone Mad

At the moment there was none, but Shannon, in his haste to be gone, almost ran down a man coming toward him up the ramp.

He swerved sharply to avoid collision, and gained a confused impression of a stocky, middle-aged man with stiff gray hair and startled light eyes in a square, weathered face.

Shock turned him cold when the man called his name: "Shannon!"

There was no question of waiting. Shannon ran past him, the gray concrete of the ramp blurring underfoot.

At the curb a private car waited, turbomotor idling, in open defiance of the brass No PARKING sign inlaid in the sidewalk. A young woman in mannish brown coveralls waited at the wheel, watching his flight with wide eyes.

A cab darted in. Shannon ran for it with the man's voice calling urgently after him: "Shannon, wait!"

The girl in the car leaned from her window, taking up the cry. "Let the cab go, Mr. Shannon! You don't understand—"

He swung aboard the cab and was gone. The vehicle's rear-view mirror gave him a glimpse of his pursuer climbing into his own car, red-faced and winded.

Twice during the trip he looked back, but the tailing car was gone, lost in the snarl of traffic. He forgot it at once.

The Keyne house was exactly as he remembered, as he had described it a dozen times to the Kyril on his flinty Ionian hillside—an unpretentious little white dwelling with a green roof and shutters to match, flowering window-boxes setting vivid splashes of color above neatly trimmed evergreens.

He cut across the lawn and climbed the steps and pressed a trembling finger to the bell push. With the action came a confusion of memories, crowding one upon another:

Himself and Ellen home from the theater, crossing the lawn through quiet snow or soft summer darkness. The two of them on the porch, keeping to one side of the doorway to miss the hallway lights when Ellen put gentle hands on his shoulders and stood on tiptoe to kiss him good night. A hundred other little intimacies, superimposed one upon another with reminders of past delight and future promise.

31

An Earth Gone Mad

The faint, musical chime of the bell drifted through the house and echoed back. There was answering movement, a sense of footsteps felt rather than heard, the indefinable certainty of approach.

Ellen's mother opened the door.

Two years ago Myra Keyne had been a thin, faintly petulant woman, wholly absorbed in the routine of her household concerns and inclined toward impatience. Now the serenity of her face was a thing totally alien to Shannon's memory, an unhuman compounding of calm and contentment.

Until now he had not faced the possibility of Cubist Change here. The horror that had fallen upon him first at the Garrick farmhouse came back icily, clogging the words in his throat.

"It's good to see you, Paul," Myra Keyne said. She opened the door, smiling, and he saw that she was dressed in the inevitable Cubist gray. "We were delighted to hear that you had come back. We hoped you'd come to see us soon."

She led him inside, the rustle of her rough gray dress loud in the indoor silence. The tranquil feel of her presence went with them like an aura. In the living room Shannon stood dumbly, trying with dry tongue to find the words he had come four hundred million miles to say.

"Ellen?" he got out finally. "Is she—"

She nodded serenely. "Ellen is here. I'm afraid this may prove a shock to you, Paul, since you can't have been home long enough to understand what the Cubes are doing for the world."

He seized her shoulders and shook her violently. "What has happened to Ellen? Where is she?"

A door opened somewhere beyond the small central hallway. Ellen's voice came out of silence, gently pleased and composed.

"Paul! We were afraid you'd forgotten us!"

He might, for the moment, have been mad. The ache in his arms and the soft pressure of Ellen's hands against his chest made him aware finally that he was crushing her to him and that she was trying, gently and without protest, to extricate herself.

32

An Earth Gone Mad

"Ellen," he said. *"Ellen!"*

She was like a child in his hands, warmly pliant but utterly without response. The gray of her Cubist dress rustled like paper under his touch, incredibly coarse and humble under the fair hair that fell in a bright shower to her shoulders. Her eyes met his fully, stirred by compassion but mirroring nothing of his own longing.

"I waited," she said. "But you didn't come back, Paul, and everyone gave you up for dead . . . then Father died, and Mother and I couldn't bear the loneliness any longer. We went to the Cube here at Suburban Sanctuary, and after that we saw things as we were meant to see them. The Change was wonderful—it took away all our grief and resentment and made life full for us. You'll understand when you go to a Sanctuary yourself."

Shannon held her from him dumbly, watching the movement of her lips and the familiar tilt of her head and trying to understand that all his journeying toward this moment had been for nothing and that it must end here. He could not accept it as a finality; his only coherent reaction was one of defeat and a red, bitter anger.

He let her go and stood back, crushed and desolate. "How could you do it, Ellen?" he demanded. "My God, I'd rather have found you dead!"

"You don't understand," she said with smiling insistence. "This is reality, Paul. The Cubes are bringing to men the ideal they seek but never find because they never know the thing they want—peace."

"The Change *is* peace," Myra Keyne said, like one responding to a ritual. "The Plan will be served."

The silence of the house closed in, oppressively.

The same serenity was here that Shannon had felt at the Garrick farmhouse, but with a difference. They had been strangers, and their alienness had touched him only from the outside; in this house, *he* was the alien. He felt suddenly like a barbarian standing uneasily in the presence of his own dead, alone and uncertain in a place still peopled by more than memories.

"I understand too well," he said. "I've lost you, after going through two years of hell to get back to you. Is there

33

any way to reverse this thing, Ellen, and be your old self again?"

She smiled as at an importunate child.

"None of us would go back even if we could. But it needn't matter, Paul—if you really want me, go to the Servants at Suburban Sanctuary. They'll help you through the Change, and we can start again as if nothing had happened."

He shook his head. "I'd rather be a robot. I can't do it!"

Her next suggestion was infinitely revolting.

"There's another way—you can take me as I am, to do with as you choose. No one protects an individual Cubist; we're only potential votes to the Government politicians, statistics to the syndicate and scapegoats to the public. You'd have no one to answer to if you took me away."

"If I *took* you?" Shannon said, appalled. "You mean you'd go with me if I demanded it, or with anyone else who wanted you?"

"Of course," she said serenely. "There's no defiance in us, don't you see? We couldn't set peace as an ideal before the Normals if we resisted—there would be no peace if we did, and the violence would be of our making. Normals fear poverty and death—we don't, and our numbers grow because of it. Some day everyone will have made the Change, and there will be a real and lasting peace. Don't you see how simple it all is, Paul?"

He saw. Carl Garrick's words came back like an echo: ". . . *and in the end they must go to the Cubes to be at peace with themselves, and then there will be peace. Forever.*"

The enormity of it staggered him, striking the harder because it was Ellen who presented the theme in all its monstrous simplicity and because Ellen was, literally, his world. He tried to imagine a people so emotionally becalmed, all ancient boundaries and ideologies erased as if they had never been, all human striving subsided into serene and smiling stagnation.

Over it all the Cubes—whatever they were, their cryptic intentions never made plain—would rule. He conceived of the thing then for the first time as a plot, a cabal not contrived by men but laid somewhere in far alien darkness, an

34

insidious Trojan Horse invasion spreading like a blight and silencing all it touched.

He could not grasp it in full complexity, but still he sensed the threat of an abstract so paradoxically fatal to humanity as an absolute and universal peace. And because Shannon was the kind of man who in order to believe in himself must first believe in something greater, he put aside his old intent and shouldered a new one, coupling native idealism to the raw hurt of his loss.

"It won't do," he said. "It's beyond reason—we can't let a thing like this happen to the world!"

"You feel lost," Ellen said, "because you can't imagine what the Cubes offer. Paul, will you let the Servants show you what it means to be free and whole?"

"I'll see them," Shannon said. His intention took shape, patterned out of anger and the bitter need of evening the score. "God, yes, I'll see them—in due time!"

He left them smiling gently at his fury, and went out of the house like a man fleeing a trap.

Outside the morning was still young, impossibly fresh and bright with sunshine and birdsong and crisp early-summer lawns. A surface car with two passengers waited at the curb, motor idling so quietly that Shannon would have passed unnoticing if the man beside the driver had not called out to him.

"Mr. Shannon! Will you talk to us now?"

Shannon halted, recognizing his gray-haired pursuer of Suburban terminal. The man opened the door, giving him his first real sight of the girl at the wheel.

She was tall, with dark hair and eyes that contrasted strongly with the indoor fairness of her skin, her most notable attraction a deep-breasted, round-limbed strength that defied the clumsy coveralls. She met Shannon's stare impersonally except for a faint tightening of her wide, full mouth.

"I am Dace Nugent," the man said. "My daughter, Ruth. Will you trust yourself with us for a time, Mr. Shannon?"

Shannon shrugged. For the moment he was without purpose or direction; these two he took for visinews collectors, but the prospect of their curiosity did not dismay him now. He might learn as much as he told.

35

He climbed into the car. "If you can tell me what has happened to the world, I'll go anywhere you say."

They were well into the outskirts of Boston Suburban when he spoke again, dredging up a question that had puzzled him subconsciously since his entrance into the Keyne house.

"Everyone seems to know I've come back," he said. "How? For that matter, how did you know to pick me up here?"

Nugent gave him a curious look. "Your return was something of a scoop for the morning visinews, and your story interested us. We've an offer to make you, Mr. Shannon, when we've time to talk."

"You knew where I'd go from the terminal," Shannon said. "Did you know what I'd find at the Keyne house, too?"

Nugent looked uncomfortable. "Yes. I checked into your past pretty thoroughly after hearing your visicast, and learned that your fiancee had turned Cubist. We could have softened the shock of your meeting if you had talked to us earlier at the—"

"My visicast?" Shannon cut in, startled.

He understood then that another move had been made in the cryptic game that had begun at Brighton, and the knowledge discouraged him from further questions.

"Never mind details now," he said wearily. "They'd only confuse me. . . Will you take me to a place where I can get a drink while we talk? I haven't had a drink for two years, and I need one."

CHAPTER FIVE

THEY DID NOT take him to a bar but to a factory-like grouping of corrugated iron buildings that huddled behind a barbed metal fence at the edge of town. A guard passed them through a formidable gate; they followed a circuitous drive that led between shops clangorous with noise, and drew up at a smaller building—of wooden construction this time—at the center of the enclosure.

One half the western area beyond was free of buildings,

forming a wide apron of reinforced concrete, and on the apron lay the ship.

Shannon stared at it curiously, puzzled and a little amused by its unorthodox design: a great coppery cylinder three hundred feet long and a third as high, sunlight glaring back from the polished curves of its horizontal hull. It had no ports, but a cryptic ring of transparent blisters at either end. There were no jets.

A slight, sandy-haired man came out of the smaller building to meet them, a long roll of blueprints furled under his arm. He was dressed carelessly in soiled brown trousers and open-necked shirt, and engine grime smudged the lines of his blunt-featured face. His eyes studied Shannon without interest, but brightened eloquently when he looked at Ruth Nugent.

The girl asked directly, "How were the field driver tests, Alec? Was there any sign of interwarp backlash?"

He shook his head, smiling. "Better than we hoped. She's ready for a trial run any time."

Dace Nugent said soberly, "I'm afraid that it will be sooner than we like. Time—" He caught himself up to make belated introduction: "Alec Blair, Paul Shannon. . . . Alec is our white hope in this project, Mr. Shannon, our physical engineer and commander of the ship once she's launched. You'll be working with him closely if you like our offer."

Shannon and Blair nodded, measuring each other. Except for his interest in Ruth Nugent, Blair struck Shannon as the dry and patient sort, obviously expert in his line but more cautious than forceful outside it.

"Welcome to our hegira, Mr. Shannon," Blair said. "I think you'll be glad, later, that you joined us."

"I haven't joined you," Shannon said. "As a matter of fact, I've no idea what this is about."

The Nugents got out of the car, forestalling Blair's answer. Shannon, finding Ruth beside him, felt an unexpected stir of interest; she was taller than either her father or Blair, so close to his own height that their eyes were almost level. In more feminine dress, he thought, she might have been quite attractive.

Nugent moved toward the building. "You'll be in for

37

lunch, Alec? We've still to explain our project to Mr. Shannon, and we may need you."

Blair nodded and disappeared into the nearest shop with his blueprints. Shannon followed the Nugents inside, and was surprised to find himself not in an office but in the sitting room of a hastily built living quarters.

The place was small but comfortable; a doorway at one end opened into a kitchen, and at the other a stairway led to sleeping rooms above.

Nugent sighed and packed a stubby pipe. "Will you bring us that drink now, Ruth? I think Shannon is going to need it when he learns what we're proposing."

The drink was cool and satisfying, the chair in which Shannon sat was infinitely comfortable. Together they made him more than ever conscious of his weariness, but did nothing to relax his wariness. He was on strange ground again, and there had been too much already that he did not understand.

"You told me in the car," he said, "that you had checked my past and found that my fiancee had turned Cubist. Will you go on from there?"

Nugent studied his drink, and the knuckles of his hand turned pale. "First let me say that we understand your situation better than you suppose. My wife—Ruth's mother—made the same Change fifteen months ago. We have not seen her for more than a year."

Ruth came in from the kitchen and refilled their glasses. She had rolled up the sleeves of her coveralls to bare round white arms, and her hair was bound back with a bit of ribbon.

"You may as well tell him the rest," she said. "If he joins us he'll know eventually, anyway."

She turned on Shannon almost angrily. "We've lived in this place for a year because we couldn't bear our own house without Mother there. We brought her home from Ohio Peace Center when her training was up, but she didn't stay. She . . . disappeared."

Nugent put down his glass, his hands under control again. "She was kidnaped, Shannon, by one of the rings that specialize in the sale of Cubists, mostly women, to the tropical

38

countries. I found my wife eventually and tried to bring her back, but she stuck to her Cubist submission and refused extradition."

Ruth turned from them to look at a framed photograph on the wall. Shannon, following her glance, saw that it was not a woman's picture but a craggy Moonscape, with the slender spire of an old-style spaceship outlined against a background of black crater-mouths and bleak mountains. Tiny figures stood about the ship, airsuits billowed out against the no-pressure of space.

It was an old picture, and very familiar—the ship was the *Prometheus*, first to break man's planetary bondage.

"I am telling you this, Mr. Shannon," Nugent's voice said harshly, "painful as it is, to demonstrate how earnest we are in our project, and to show why we must escape from Earth before it is too late."

When Shannon said nothing, he went on doggedly. "There is less protection for Cubists in other countries than in the States, and in some they are sold like cattle. My wife is, and has been since her abduction, an inmate of a Colombian brothel."

He studied Shannon intently, weighing his reaction. "It can happen to your fiancee, or to anyone who makes the Change, and there is nothing that can be done about it."

Shannon said stiffly, "Government—"

"Is not interested in individual Cubists," Nugent said. "Government has its hands full with Cubism as an issue. You've a great deal to learn, and the first is that you can't oppose complete submission—no one can, and that includes Government."

His certainty chilled Shannon and at the same time angered him. "Then I'll guard Ellen myself. I'll bring her out of that damned trance if there's a possible way, and if there isn't—"

Nugent cut him off wearily. "You'll start a personal crusade? It's a hopeless contest. The only answer is to run, to run as far and as fast as we must to escape total ruin."

Shannon held his temper with an effort. "I think you give up too easily."

Ruth Nugent turned to face him with a curious pride.

"We haven't given up," she said. "We're taking the only course left us." She looked back to the photograph. "My grandfather built that ship, and my father built the *Icarus*, the first to reach Mars. But they were nothing, compared to the one we're building now."

Shannon looked at Nugent with new respect. "So you're *that* Nugent! Under different circumstances, sir, I'd feel it an honor to be here."

"But as it is, you're more curious than pleased," Nugent said. "And more disturbed than curious. So is the rest of the world, except for the Cubists and our little handful who staff the *Ark*."

"The *Ark*? Is that symbolism?"

"And more," Nugent said. "Earth is a lost world, Shannon. And Man is a lost race—I know how melodramatic this sounds, but it's true—if the *Ark* fails. A few of us realized over a year ago what is coming, and we launched this project to save as much of the race as may prove worth saving. The *Ark* is the first stellar ship ever built. It will probably be the last, since we're setting out nine days from now for Alpha Canis Minoris—Procyon."

"Procyon?" Shannon stared, tempted to laugh outright. "If you were anyone else, I'd say you were mad. Procyon is eleven light-years—"

"I didn't bring you here to teach me stellar distances," Nugent interrupted him. "I'm offering you a berth with our expedition. The *Ark* is well staffed already, but we're mostly specialists and technicians in skills that make for poor frontiersmen. We need an experienced man to head colonizing parties, and a structural engineer who knows the emergencies of colonial life. You fit both categories, Mr. Shannon. It needs a hard and resourceful man to live two years off Earth."

Shannon shook his head. "I think you *are* mad."

Nugent shrugged. "They said the same when my father built the *Prometheus*. But it's time for interstellar flight. There's a pressing need for it, and it's within our reach.

"Procyon supports a planetary system—the Maxon-Bell spectral analysis proved that years ago. It's a double star, which is unfortunate, but is younger than Sol and has at
40

least twelve planets large enough to support life. We have a completely new propulsion principle that approaches the speed of light—we're equipped and provisioned for a twelve-year passage, and we have every expectation of making the trip safely."

Shannon finished his drink, his incredulity waning before the older man's assurance. In his field, Nugent was a power; in spite of himself Shannon felt a stir of interest in the picture built up before him. If the chance had come two years ago—

"We've gone into this choice thoroughly," Nugent said. "Alpha Centauri is nearer than Procyon, but its three-body system of revolution rules it out—its planets would be climatic madhouses. Sirius is too massive and hot, Epsilon Eridani and 61 Cygni too small. Altair has no planetary system."

He turned to Ruth. "Will you bring the *Ark*'s equipage book from the safe? I'd like to show Mr. Shannon our data on animation-suspension for the older members."

Ruth hesitated. "I don't think you should, Father. The light-drive components are in it too, and—"

"Don't bother," Shannon said, irritated by her distrust. "I'm not interested in the flight. If I'd known what you wanted of me, I wouldn't have come here in the first place."

She turned on him angrily. "And why shouldn't you go, Mr. Shannon? What can you do here?"

"A great deal," he said. "There's my fiancee, and others like her. I couldn't desert Ellen in this madhouse if I wanted to."

"There's nothing anyone can do. We've proved that, painfully, with my mother."

Nugent intervened quickly. "Alec will be in shortly. Ruth, will you make lunch for us while I bring Mr. Shannon up to date? I promised to tell him about the Cubes, you know."

His third drink, and his near exhaustion, made Shannon a little drunk. He sat with the empty glass cold in his hand, only half hearing Nugent's voice through a blue haze of pipe smoke while he puzzled over his own concerns.

Thoughts slipped through his awareness like fish through a clouded pool, evading his grasp. Before he realized it he

41

was at grips again with the fantastic riddle that had drawn him in, probing for the core of sense that must be in it and finding none.

In the kitchen, Ruth Nugent made efficient bustling sounds; the smell of coffee and the crackle of a high-frequency oven came to him. Her father's voice droned on, resuming intelligibility only when Shannon gave up his problem for the hundredth time and settled himself reluctantly to listen.

". . that we failed to identify either their origin or nature is proof enough that we're not equipped to fight the Cubes," Nugent was saying. "Something might have been done at first, when people still joked about them and called them star dice, but the things are under Government protection now. It's ironic, isn't it, that the republican principle must defend any principle so important to a large number of people, no matter how subversive it may be. And the followers of the Cubes have grown so many that the end is already in sight for those who have brains to see it. We've rushed construction of the *Ark* to finish ahead of that day.

"Abandoning Earth is our only hope. You'll see that, Shannon."

Admitting the man's earnestness, Shannon automatically discounted the cogency of his argument. Nugent was an idealist with an axe to grind; his father had built the first ship that paved the way for terrestrial expansion, and he was bent on carrying that tradition to the stars. To prove his point he was willing to undertake a flight that might endure even beyond his lifetime, and to take with him any whom he might convince.

A more immediate interest occurred to Shannon, rousing him to wariness again. "You mentioned a visicast I'm supposed to have made, but you didn't explain. Are the police looking for me?"

Nugent, pouring another drink, stopped to stare. "Police? My God, man, you're a hero, not a fugitive!"

He refilled Shannon's glass and said curiously, "You baffle me, Shannon. Why should the civil authorities want you?"

When Shannon hesitated, he said apologetically: "Sorry—

forget that I asked. But there's one thing I'd like to know, if I may."

He packed his stubby pipe again. "Landing a jury-rigged ship like that little runabout of yours so close to destination was a phenomenal bit of navigation. How did you manage, with so many instruments smashed?"

"So close?" Shannon repeated. It had not been close; he had been lucky to strike the right hemisphere. From Denver to—

Caution stopped the words in his mouth. "Where did they find the *Flora?*"

Nugent's answer shocked him horribly. "In an abandoned field just outside Boston Metro. No one knew where you had gone until you turned up on the morning visicast. . . . I imagine Solar Services was behind your refusal to tell where you spent those two years."

"I didn't refuse," Shannon said numbly. At grips with this latest inconsistency, he was hardly conscious of answering. "I was on Io."

Nugent stood up abruptly. "*Io!* Ruth, did you hear?"

Ruth came out of the kitchen, her face flushed from the heat. "I heard. And I don't believe it."

The exchange between them brought Shannon out of his funk. "What's so strange about my being marooned on Io?"

Nugent said hastily, "Unusual would be a better word. Io is a wild and terrible place—Ruth and I were there with Alec a few years ago, exploring for radioactives, and we found it all but uninhabitable even with full equipment. It's hard to believe that a man could exist there for two weeks, let alone two years."

His sudden interest and denial only added another dubious piece to an already senselessly complicated puzzle.

"I think you're lying," Shannon said. He stood up, his earlier irritation fanned to anger. "I don't know or care why, but it doesn't matter. I've heard nothing but lies and defeatism since I came back, and I'm sick of it."

He put down his glass to go, and halted when the door opened against his hand. Alec Blair came in, his sandy hair carefully brushed and the smudge of soot scoured from his blunt-featured face. Shannon met the steady regard of the superintendent's light eyes and felt an icy dislike in them that matched his own.

"Stand out of my way," Shannon said. "I'm going out."

The whiskey he had drunk warmed him and sent a hot surge of recklessness flooding through him. He wanted suddenly to wipe out his frustration in violence, to lay hands on something he could twist and break and exhaust his dammed-up resentment on.

Blair closed the door, ignoring his order. "I thought you were going to tame the new worlds for us. Don't tell me you've lost your stomach for adventure already!"

"It's not a matter of nerve," Shannon said. His anger burned the higher because he recognized it for what it was, a defensive reaction denying his uncertainty. "It's an issue of doing what I can to help mend the damage that fools and cowards have done by tolerating those damned Cubes."

Ruth Nugent came between them, her own eyes angry. "You're behaving like a child, Shannon. You've set yourself against a thing too big to fight, and you're shouting at us because you're afraid—afraid to face the truth."

His face went hot. "And I think you're a bunch of spineless fatalists. Your only solution is to run like rats from a sinking ship."

She bit her lip in sudden hurt. "Do you think we'd desert my mother, if anything could be done?"

She was suddenly shaken and defenseless, competence shattered to discover a softness that Shannon found infinitely appealing. But his anger had swept him too far; he wanted to stop before he hurt her further, and could not.

"Wouldn't you?" he said.

Blair's hand on his shoulder swung him about. "That's enough, Shannon. Get out."

Shannon caught his wrist, jerked him off balance and flung him crashing to the floor at Ruth Nugent's feet.

"I didn't ask to be brought here," he said. "I think your project is a fool's errand and a coward's compromise. I don't want any part of it, now or ever."

He shut the door forcibly behind him, leaving them to stare at each other helplessly. Alec Blair got up from the

44

floor, his blunt face ruddy with anger, and brushed at his clothing.

"How much did you tell him, Dace?" he demanded. "Did he see the light-drive components?"

"Of course not," Ruth said. She went to him quickly and put a hand on his shoulder. "Don't mind this, Alec. We're lucky to lose him."

"He didn't listen to the little I told him," Nugent said placatingly. "He's in a desperate frame of mind just now, Alec. I can't say that I blame him for what happened."

Blair said shortly, "The man's a damned maniac."

Nugent disagreed. "Have you thought how you'd feel if you came home to find your fiancee a Cubist, and no one doing anything about it? You'd be bitter too, I think."

He sighed when they stood together, denying him in silence. "The fact remains that we need him, whether we like him or not. I think he'll be back once he learns what he's set himself against—if he doesn't kill himself first."

They let it rest at that.

CHAPTER SIX

THE FIRST turbobus to pass the Nugent plant took Shannon back to Boston Suburban and to a helicab that dropped him in the Metro area. The anger in him had not died; he let it take its course, finding a perverse relief in the violence he had forced. Once he felt a brief touch of shame when he remembered Ruth Nugent's stricken look, and banished it by turning to his dilemma again.

He was no nearer to a solution than before. Rather, instead of discovering a thread of reason for his position, he found himself sinking deeper into a quagmire of senseless contradictions. Only one certainty emerged—before he could help Ellen he must learn a great deal more, and he could trust only one person to tell him the truth.

He was still considering his first step when the turbobus dropped him in the rush and bustle of downtown Metro, and he felt for the first time the real undercurrent of tension that drove the thronging crowds.

An Earth Gone Mad

It was not a sense to be defined precisely, but it left him disturbed and vaguely uneasy: a febrile anxiety in some that lent a tight-drawn look, a slackness of indifference in others, a too-bright recklessness in the eyes of a few that had in it nothing of gaiety. And he realized presently that he had never seen so many beggars—the hangdog, dissolute sort that had all but disappeared before his exile.

There was a general carelessness of dress, a new and puzzling shabbiness. He passed bars surprisingly busy for so early an afternoon hour, places blatant with overloud music and jostling with unsteady celebrants. From the open doorway of one such place a young girl, glass in hand, called to him shrilly above the din.

Shannon shrugged and passed on, but in his present mood the girl's immature abandon stuck in his mind, her prostituted youth fitting with disquieting aptness into the atmosphere of dissolution he sensed about him. In a society better coordinated, he thought, such a thing could not happen; but it had always been so, and therefore men must have been wrong, somehow, from the beginning.

He sighted the soaring spire of the Solar Services building then, and his depression lifted, bringing purpose out of uncertainty—he needed money as well as information for his fight, and Solar would have both.

The place was identically the same as other Solar buildings, but larger than most. He went up the broad ramp toward the columned facade, and wondered suddenly if he would be stopped again as he had been stopped in Denver.

But no one waited for him under the entrance arch nor in the long lobby beyond. He went through the busy first floor with its rows of information booths and banks of radophone cubicles, and entered an elevator leading to administration levels above.

The cage slid smoothly up, lending a feeling of being at last on familiar ground that made him almost cheerful until he saw that the lift operator was a gray-clad Cubist.

The man waited in smiling patience, hand on the selector stud. "Your floor, sir?"

"Personnel," Shannon said automatically.

He watched the man curiously, recalling the disjointed

46

gabble he had heard from the visinews machine at Metro terminal. Doubt shook his old confidence in Solar's judgment.

"So Solar *is* hiring your kind," he said.

The operator nodded placidly. "More than any other syndicated utility, sir. They find our services very satisfactory."

The cage door opened on a carpeted hallway that stretched between even rows of frosted office doors. "I saw your morning visicast, Mr. Shannon," the operator said. "I'm sure you'll feel differently when you understand the Cubes better."

"Visicast?"

He remembered then: someone had impersonated him long enough that morning to give a bogus interview to the press—and why not? If the players behind the scene could transport the *Flora* to Boston Metro and transfer him as forcibly after her, the impersonation was only a small step further in the same plot.

He wondered briefly what words *they* might have put into his mouth, and gave up speculating at once because he felt that the answer to that one puzzle, at least, was within his reach.

He left the elevator and went down the corridor to a door marked *Salaried Personnel*. Entering, the instant hush that fell across the busy room told him that he was expected.

Half the office force were Cubists.

A tall blonde girl with a secretary's unmistakable efficiency came toward him from an inner door marked *M. Clayton, Superintendent*.

"Mr. Clayton is expecting you," she said.

He followed her, and forgot her at once when the man at the desk looked up sharply at his entrance. Clayton was a short, heavy man with a balding head and pince-nez clamped over light, cold eyes. He did not rise to meet Shannon; instead he placed a visinews digest sheet on the desk and touched its featured column with a manicured finger.

"Now that you've condescended to visit us," he said acidly, "will you explain why you gave this interview without first consulting us?"

47

An Earth Gone Mad

Shannon took the sheet curiously and found a tri-di cut of his own face staring back at him, the expression set and angry. The caption above the picture said blackly:

RETURNED SOLAR ENGINEER SHOCKED BY
CHANGES—DENOUNCES CUBIST TREND

There followed a terse account of his appearance in Boston Metro at nine o'clock of the same morning, and of the trenchant attack he had made upon Cubism before representatives of Interworld Visicasts.

He had, as Nugent had said, made no statement as to where he had been marooned. Asked his opinion of the Cubist crisis, he had reacted with mounting bitterness, citing his own loss of Ellen; at the end, he had thrown discretion to the winds and denounced Government's failure to curb Cubism. He had gone so far as to advocate force—the Workers' Guild, he declared, showed the only real awareness of danger he had met with. "I pray that all patriotic, all thinking citizens will support the Guild in its crusade. . . ."

Side columns presented variations of the main story, with speculations by uneasy commentators as to the effect his incendiary plea might have upon a public already restless and inflamed.

Shannon read the lot of it, and found it damning.

They had been ahead of him again, maneuvering him to suit their own purposes, committing him to a stand not of his own choosing and forestalling any contrary tack he might have taken.

He put down the paper to meet Clayton's glare.

"You wouldn't believe me if I denied this," he said. "And since I agree with it except for Guild action, I see no reason why I should. I think the world has gone stark mad."

The personnel manager purpled. "You had no right to make such statements, Shannon! You've ruined your standing with Solar—your contract will be canceled. You'll never find another engineer's berth without our recommendation."

"The blacklist," Shannon said.

48

An Earth Gone Mad

He was mildly amazed to find how far his two years of fighting Io's harsh environment had undermined his respect for authority. Solar Services had once been the natural arbiter of his opinion and action, and in the turn of a moment it had become no more than a minor and expendable quantity.

"I'll get by," he said, "on the back wages you owe me."

"It's hardly as simple as that," Clayton said. His voice took on a grim relish. "You're not discharged yet, but neither are you cleared. The decision rests with President Orsham."

In spite of himself, Shannon felt a touch of bitter humor at the man's patent satisfaction. Wherever Solar reached, Orsham's name was a word used with care, sworn by as a sort of substitute deity, his personal attention the ultimate threat.

"Then let's get on with it," Shannon said.

A buzzer sounded peremptorily on Clayton's desk. Clayton said hastily, "At once, sir!" and motioned Shannon curtly to an inner office beyond.

They found Orsham waiting at a massive desk, flanked by a nervous male secretary and two guards in street clothing. Shannon had seen the Solar president only in visicasts before, and his first sight of the great man now left him puzzled and faintly disappointed. Orsham was a slighter and less impressive personage than he had expected—there was a certain dignity in the narrow face and cold eyes, but little of the weight and power Shannon had anticipated.

Orsham came immediately to the business at hand.

"From your remarks to Mr. Clayton," he said, "I inferred that you might deny having made the visicast in question, on the grounds of being impersonated. By whom, may I ask?"

"I've no idea," Shannon said. "I hadn't intended to bother making a denial. I've business of my own to look after, and I see no point in wasting the time."

Clayton and Orsham's secretary exchanged shocked glances. Orsham nodded without expression.

"You hold a responsible position with us, Shannon. Think carefully before you discard it."

49

Impatience goaded Shannon. "I'm quite ready to give it up."

"But we feel responsible, in a sense, for your deprivation," Orsham persisted. "Solar will keep you on its rolls, Shannon, on condition that you repudiate the visicast made in your name. As it stands, it is too damaging to ignore. A public denial—"

Shannon rose abruptly, his mind made up. He had been a pawn in this game from the beginning—Orsham's offer would leave him more a catspaw than ever. No engineer's defiance could be important enough to bring the head of a syndicate to terms; Orsham wanted him for another, less obvious, reason.

"I'm not interested," Shannon said. "If you'll give me a draft to the amount of my salary, I'll call it even and go."

Orsham nodded to the gaping Clayton. "Pay him," he said.

CHAPTER SEVEN

THE FEVERISH tension of the crowds must have had its effect on him, Shannon thought. Until a few minutes ago his break with Solar had been unconsidered and unforeseen, but now, leaving his career behind him, he felt neither regret nor concern.

He made his way toward the nearest remembered bank, jostled by the crowds but only half conscious of the press about him. The certainty that someone had impersonated him kept recurring, and he turned the problem over in his mind as he walked, searching for a reason behind the deception.

Someone had used his name and face to separate him neatly from his job, setting him willy-nilly on a course deliberately designed to identify him publicly·as an enemy of the Cubes—and as a supporter of the Workers' Guild in its fight to suppress Cubism.

The Guild! The informative crackle of the terminal visi-news machine came back to him, for the second time, point-

ing up his sudden surmise: *"Guild Head Zimmer Conniston
.   ultimatum to Government   . industrial shutdown unless hiring of Cubists is halted .   ."*

He cursed himself for not having understood earlier. A
Guild powerful enough to stand against both Solar and
Government was also strong enough to maneuver him into
any position it desired.

How it had been done did not greatly matter; paradoxically, the simple knowledge that he had been tricked left
him relieved rather than angered.

There was, after all, a pattern of logic running through
and sustaining the whole improbable muddle. Once he
found Gil and learned more answers, he might be able to
act on his own initiative instead of being twitched like a
puppet through a routine already determined for him.

Reaching the bank, he found it closed for the afternoon.
He retraced his steps, pondering his next move. Should he
try to find Gil now?

The doors of a bar swung inward ahead of him, letting
out a man who blinked against the afternoon brightness
and moved unsteadily away. A burst of sound followed him
from inside and was shut off by the closing door, a confused
mingling of voices above insistent music, the shuffling of
feet and tinkle of glasses.

It was the same bar Shannon had passed earlier on his
way to Solar Services. He shrugged and turned in. He had
to take time out, somewhere, to think—why not here?

He pushed through the crowd to a quieter corner, found
an empty booth and pressed the signal stud set in the wall
beside the service grill. When the little bulb glowed he
gave his order, deposited a coin in the slot and waited for
his drink to appear through the table's hollow supporting
column.

The taste of it, when it came, reminded him of his morning with the Nugents.

He cast back over the short time he had spent with them,
stirring uncomfortably when he recalled the manner of his
leaving, and finished with a conclusion that surprised him.
Their defeatism still jarred, but he found himself admitting
honestly that they, of all the people he had met since his

51

An Earth Gone Mad

return, had grasped a practical way out of the trap in which the world was caught.

Practical—but to run without hope of return, leaving everything familiar and valued behind . .

Movement and the smell of cheap perfume made him look up irritably to see that a girl was taking the seat across from him in the booth. She met his scowl with gamin assurance and pressed the signal stud for a drink.

"I'm glad you came back," she said. "I called you when you passed earlier, but you didn't hear."

He recalled the incident without interest. "Why call to me when there are so many others here already?"

She laughed and caught the glass that slid up to her hand. "Because you're not like these others. I'm sick of them, and you're interesting."

She was even younger than he had first supposed. Under its cosmetic veneer her skin was still smooth and clear, contrasting oddly with her too-dark brows and improbably tinted hair. The dress she wore had never been meant for the street, a clinging filmy thing cut deliberately low to display small, immature breasts.

"Interesting?" Shannon said. He shifted restlessly, wanting to be rid of her and at the same time intrigued by something searching and pathetic in her lightness.

"Different, then. Everyone else is drifting, waiting for something to happen, and when it does happen they don't know what it means. You know what you want."

He frowned, impressed in spite of himself by her instinctive summation of the crowd-spirit that had so puzzled him. She was quite in earnest, and the eyes above her painted smile were clear and deeply distressed.

"What about yourself?" he asked. He was suddenly and intensely interested, feeling an unaccountable certainty that he was closer to the truth than he had been since his return. "Are you drifting, or are you sure of what you want?"

She laughed, a practiced rattle of sound utterly at discord with her eyes. "I'm drifting. The world is going to hell—but who am I to tell it to stop? I'm waiting like the rest of them, for the blowup."

She finished her drink and pressed the signal stud. When

52

her glass reappeared, she lifted it to Shannon in sudden defiance.

"And what's the difference if I drift? If the going gets too rough, there's always the Cubes—and they offer one thing you can't get anywhere else nowadays. Peace."

Shannon said curiously, understanding her perfectly and wondering at his ability to understand: "That's what I've felt, without naming it, in everyone since I came back. Drink and be merry—and to hell with the piper. The Servants will always take you in."

"That's it. It's not like religion—you don't have to be sorry about anything, you just go to them and let them take care of the rest. Nothing matters after that because you're happy, because you can't *help* being happy."

She pressed the signal stud a third time.

Waiting for the drink, she looked at Shannon with new interest. "Since you came back, you said. I know you, now —you're Shannon, the man who was marooned out in the asteroids!"

She leaned toward him when he did not answer. "I missed your visicast, but I heard the talk of it. The Guild is playing it up big—Conniston and his crew are getting ready to fight, and they're using your case to raise the public against the Cubes."

The drink rose between her hands, but she ignored it.

"Don't let them use you, Shannon. You haven't been touched by the rot that's eating the heart out of the rest of us! You can't fight it, but you can get out—"

A heavy man with too-pink skin and carefully curled white hair came out of the confusion and dropped the girl's drink, glass and all, into the disposal chute. The girl shrank from him.

"You've had enough," the man said. "Get upstairs."

She loosed her rattling laugh when Shannon stood up with her. "For God's sake don't play Galahad here. I work in this place."

"You don't have to," Shannon said. "The Cubes would be better."

She moved away, body swaying in an exaggerated rhythm that still had in it something of coltish, adolescent awkward-

53

ness. The man paused briefly, measuring Shannon with colorless eyes, before following her.

Shannon went out without finishing his drink.

The place had become suddenly like a sty, acrawl with gross motion and reeking with excess. The early evening air was cool on his face; a part of the day's throng had gone with the sun, but the comparative quiet did nothing to relieve the depression that had fallen upon him in the bar.

He moved through the thinning crowds like a man dazed, caught up in a bitter wonder at the world and at himself.

A part of what he had felt since his return was traceable to the Cubes, but not all—the rest was Man's own. The girl in the bar was not the first of her kind, nor the last. The coming of the Cubes had only brought to a head the ugly unfinishedness of men that had driven them wrong from the beginning.

But if it had been like this always, why should he realize the truth of it now? Why should it all seem so significant and at the same time so desperately hopeless?

Is this what the prophets warned us against? he wondered. *Is there a basic rottenness in the race that grows with numbers, and a will to destruction that made us a slow failure from the start?*

He did not know how long he wandered in the streets, lost in speculation entirely foreign to his usual cast of thought. It seemed to him that he must have circled the same block many times, since he retained a vague memory of having passed more than once the bar he had left.

Another place, in midblock across the street, caught his eye with each passing. Its unadorned simplicity, standing out in quiet relief among its garishly neoned neighbors, brought him finally to a halt for a better look.

He felt a cold shock of excitement when he realized what place it was.

The narrow white facade bore no identification beyond a small greenish emblem set high up in the center, a three-dimensional block that fluoresced strongly enough against rival neons to illuminate the single word chiseled above the arched, double-doored entrance: Sanctuary.

There would be a Cube inside. Shannon went directly

54

across the street, disregarding the angry honking of traffic, his whole awareness centered on the fact that here, at last, was a Cube.

He had to face them sooner or later. Why not now?

It seemed to him when he mounted the curb that the stream of passersby slowed briefly before the double doors, that every face wore for the moment of passage a transient look of peace. A loose group of spectators watched from the side, some patently curious, some staring with a fixity that ignored outside sound and action.

The girl he had met in the bar came out of the group and stood before Shannon, so close that he could smell the heavy perfume she affected. The greenish glow of the fluorescence overhead made her face paler than ever under its mask of cosmetics; her eyes, dark and enormous, were full of terror and a strange ecstasy.

"You were right," she said. "The Cubes *are* better than what I had back there. . I've tried twice before to go in, and couldn't. Tonight I can."

She looked at the waiting group that skirted the doorway. "They come here every night, most of them, like suicides wanting to die but afraid to take the step. They want the peace they know is in there, but they're afraid of that, too. I was afraid of it once, but not any more. To be quiet—"

She moved away. At the entrance she looked back and saw that Shannon was following, and made an urgent gesture of negation.

"You don't need this," she said. "Go away!"

She went quickly into the arched entranceway without looking back. The doors opened, swallowed her up into a green inner gloom and closed without a sound.

Shannon felt rather than heard the sigh that swept the watching crowd. He was within arm's reach of the doors when he felt the pull of the place—a soothing aura of euphoric calm that evoked vividly the quality he had felt first in the Garricks and then in Ellen. Contentment. Peace, serenity and utter resignation.

He stopped to grapple with a sudden conviction that until this moment he had been victim to a terrible misconception, that there was no possible evil inside but a blessed relief from all uncertainties that plagued him. He had been wrong from the beginning in his hatred of the Cubes. . . .

Simultaneously he was aware that the crowd watched him with cat-and-mouse intensity. The weight of their regard brought a counter conviction that they had seen others come before him to struggle for their identity, and to fail.

The doors swung open.

A bearded old man in a plain gray robe stood in the opening, smiling regretfully. Behind him in the Sanctuary gloom Shannon glimpsed a greenish glow that seemed impossibly far away for so small a place; robed figures passed before it, dimming the light with a regularity that had in it the repetitive cadence of ritual. Among them Shannon glimpsed the girl who had just entered, walking erect and serene with a child's earnest grace.

"I am sorry," the Servant said. "Some few are not acceptable to the Cubes. You are one."

The doors closed. A surprised murmur ran through the crowd.

Anger grew in him, shearing like a blade through the compulsion that held him. He reached out a rough hand toward the doors.

At his shoulder someone said authoritatively: "The Sanctuaries are under civil protection. No one enters without invitation."

He turned to face a massive young man in the green uniform of the civil patrols. The trooper's eyes were wary, and he swung a rubber truncheon suggestively.

Shannon fought down his impatience. Another time—

The crowd parted abruptly, making way for two men in civilian clothing. One held an open card-case in his hand, extended for the patrolman's inspection; the other held a shock-rod ready.

"Government," the first said. "We've had this man under surveillance for days. We're ready to take him now."

The pale blue beam of the shock-rod caught Shannon and convulsed him with the stunning agony of total neural disorganization. There was a terrifying instant when he spun bodilessly into darkness—and after that, nothing.

CHAPTER EIGHT

HE AWOKE in an intolerable glare of white light.

Someone stood over him, blurred and indistinct, holding a glass of some pungent liquid to his lips. There was a steady murmur of voices and a crepitant rustling of paper in the background.

". . . had to do it," someone said doggedly. "He'd have been detained if we hadn't stepped in. We'd have lost him."

Another voice, wonderingly: ". . . Cube field didn't stop him, even under the arch. And the Servant *refused* him!"

The one standing over Shannon answered in a dry, familiar voice that jolted Shannon out of his daze. "You shouldn't have shocked him out, though. He won't thank us for that."

Shannon got his hands under him and fought to sit up.

"Gil!" he said thickly. "Gil Lucas!"

His vision cleared slowly and he saw his friend as he had pictured him, in exile, a thousand times: a plump, short man in his early thirties, round of face and a little stooped, straw-blond hair receding toward baldness and restless light eyes half hidden behind glinting spectacles. He was smiling at the moment, showing large square teeth spaced a little apart, but even in relief there was a hint of suppressed energy about him, a spring-tense, dynamic intelligence.

He put the glass into Shannon's hand. "Drink this, Paul. It should ease the neural reaction."

The pungence of it cleared Shannon's head quickly, and he sat up to find himself in the lounge of an expensive apartment, a place of thick dull rugs and subdued paintings and tall windows heavily draped.

"I thought I'd never find you," Shannon said. "The world has gone mad, and I couldn't trust anyone. What did happen, Gil?"

"A devious story and not a pretty one," Gil said. "But I'll try to brief you before my client arrives." He turned to the other two men in the room, and Shannon saw that they

57

were the same who had taken him from the patrolman at the Sanctuary. "You're not needed any longer. Get out."

They went. Shannon stood up, feeling his strength returning and his interest with it. "Your client?"

"Zimmer Conniston," Gil said wryly. "High Chairman of the Free Guilds, self-appointed savior of Mankind and one of the two most powerful men on Earth. A brutal fool driven by the will to power, but a shrewd one—as witness his judgment in hiring me to head the only research project ever dedicated to destroying the Cubes."

He moved across the room, passing before a massive phonovision console and a crystal-paned alcove filled with figurines, to stop at an automix bar in a corner.

"Toast now, celebration later," he said. He drew two drinks, frosted and aromatic, from the robot dispenser inside.

Later they sat facing each other, smoking and relaxing in the warmth of reunion. A prismatic city-glow stained the night sky outside; through the windows floated the busy hum of traffic far below, a murmurous rhythm like the droning of a vast, half sleeping hive.

"You can understand how I felt when I saw Ellen," Shannon said. With its telling, all that had happened to him had become distant and unreal, as if he detailed the nonsense of a dream. "Gil, what is really behind all this, and what can be done about it?"

Gil sipped his drink, his round face sober.

"The six of us—Goff, Harris, Campion, Landrum, MacGuinness and I—have dug at that question for months, spending Conniston's money high and low, and we've learned nothing we didn't know already. There's no logic in it, Paul, no base for experimental analysis. Personally, I've nothing to show for my labor but a nagging premonition—you'd call it a hunch, and be right—so wild that even a telemovie fantasy show wouldn't touch it."

He shook himself and gave Shannon his wry, squaretoothed grin. "The truth is that I'm stumped, and afraid—afraid because if my hunch should prove right there'd be no hope at all. Even Dace Nugent's *Ark* might not fly far enough to escape."

"It can't be as bad as that," Shannon protested. "I've been too far from the problem—maybe you've been too close to it. Didn't anyone ever test one?"

"Dozens of them were tested when they first appeared twenty months ago, but that was before they turned active. We've assumed since that they are either intelligent after a fashion we can't identify, or are activated extensions of some intelligence we can't detect. The early laboratory analyses didn't hint at anything of the sort. They checked out as ordinary fluorspar."

"Fluorspar?"

"I've seen original data on some, though I've been damned careful never to go near a Cube. They're fluorspar, or were: simple cubic forms measuring two inches to a side, none perfectly symmetrical and giving up the usual colloidal impurities, manganese and rare-earth traces. They fluoresce in ultraviolet, have the standard hardness of 4 and specific gravity of 3.2, and they fit the regular patterns of interpenetrating calcium-fluoride lattices.

"As for their being alive, there's an analogy in carbon-based organisms; a body an instant after death is the same, physically and chemically, as it was before except for one thing—the activating spark is gone. Until we know what life is, we'll have to assume that non-carbon forms may have it too.

"It wasn't until there were thousands of the things floating about that they woke up and began their Change. After that they were brought in from everywhere, examined and passed up to higher authorities. They contaminated every mind they touched—before we realized it, the best scientific brains of the world were calling themselves Servants of the Cubes and setting up Sanctuaries.

"Specialists refused to go near the things once the danger was recognized, but by then it was too late. Today there probably are not more than a score or so of really able scientists left—if you discount Nugent's crew, which kept to itself from the start—and they're mostly mathematicians and astronomers, the sort who handle their research at second hand."

"There was a definite plan, then," Shannon said.

An Earth Gone Mad

Gil nodded wearily. "But proving it to Government is another matter. One of the evils of democracy is that nothing a large enough group of citizens want can be suppressed, and the Cubists have taken advantage of it. They're already a tremendous voting power.

"From one view, a society of Cubists wouldn't be a bad thing; it would be stable and peaceful, at least. But the trouble is now that everybody has an axe to whet and they're using the Cubists to turn the wheels—they think. Politicians and syndicates and Government itself are angling for Cubist backing, though they ignore them as individuals. And all of them refuse to understand that it's only a matter of time until there's nothing left but Cubism, when personal axes go into the scrap heap for good. You can see it: Cubists finally elected to office, reaching a majority in Government, taking over the world.

"But first there's going to be open opposition, amounting to civil war. Conniston's Guild is the only body strong enough to fight them—that's why my staff and I are willing to work with a thug like Conniston, because we see that war coming and hope to prevent it."

He sat up abruptly at the coded flashing on an annunciator bulb over the door.

"Brace yourself—here comes Conniston. He's back from a bribing expedition which I predicted wouldn't come off well, and you'll see him at his engaging worst."

The door opened. A small, pale man came in with a dart-gun in his hand, flicked the room with a glance and halted to face Shannon and Gil Lucas.

Conniston strode after him.

Shannon saw a huge, lowering man well past middle age, with a mane of stiff white hair bristling over a square-jowled face and a ponderous body running to fat. Conniston, ignoring them after a single sullen glance, went directly to the automix bar in the corner. Shannon watched him curiously, sensing the animal force and blunt, brutal arrogance of the man behind his scowling preoccupation.

"You couldn't buy MacLeod off," Gil said. "I thought not."

Conniston answered without turning, hands busy with the

60

robot dispenser. "Damn MacLeod. I can do without him."

Gil explained to Shannon: "Wilson MacLeod is Chairman of the Economic Stabilization Board. Conneston hoped to influence him against Governmental recognition of Cubists as a legal labor element, but it didn't work out that way. The financial weight was on the other side—Orsham bought him first."

Conniston's guard lounged against a chair without putting away his weapon. Conniston, his drink made, drew a cigar from a jacket pocket and puffed it alight, his pale eyes considering Lucas.

"I warned you not to handle this like an ordinary political skirmish," Gil said. "It's not even a matter of economics, at root. It's a technical problem that must be evaluated and understood before we can solve it. We've got to learn how the Cubes work, and why, and get at them without stirring up a civil disturbance that will bring Government in with the syndicates against us."

"There's only one way to handle this," Conniston said through a curl of blue smoke. "I've avoided it before on your advice, Lucas, but I'm ready to use it now."

"I know," Gil said. "Force." He shook his head, and the light danced on his thick lenses. "I expected you'd come to that eventually, because it's the only line you understand. But force won't work, Conniston—bombing the Sanctuaries will only kill innocent people, and when the smoke clears the Cubes won't have been touched. You'll make martyrs of the Servants and turn Government and the public against you."

"You had your chance to produce," Conniston said. "You and your theorists, but you only talked and spent money. I'm through marking time. So are you."

Unexpectedly, Gil laughed. "We foresaw this, too. Predicting your reactions was light work, Conniston—you started life as a muscler and you can't shake the conditioning. You can't win without my crew; don't underestimate us!"

"You underestimate *me*," Conniston said. He nodded to his man, who stood up expectantly, dart-gun ready. "Did you foresee this, too?"

Gil gave Shannon a glance that warned: *Stay out of this.*

"Long ago," he said, and finished his drink without haste. "Your psychology dates straight back to the Paleolithic, Conniston. We took it for granted that when our first research failed to show quick results—and an immediate solution was out of the question from the beginning—you'd try to eliminate us. Once you can't use us any longer, we're dangerous. We know too much of your plans."

Conniston settled his thick shoulders like a wrestler. "Then you're a fool. You waited too long to pull out."

"We waited long enough to give you a chance to work out a peaceful solution," Gil said. "But we've been prepared against this decision of yours for weeks. There's a portable tapecaster hidden in your automix bar. Every word of this conversation—and of a dozen others—is on file in the hands of my staff."

Conniston reached the automix in two ponderous strides, smashing aside bottles and glasses when he flung it open. He glared for a moment at the tiny tapecaster unit in his hand, and flung it in sudden speechless fury to the floor.

"One other thing," Gil said above the jangle of breaking ceramics. "Paul and I are no Cubist nonentities. If we fail to show up tomorrow this story goes to Government, and even a High Chairman of the Guilds will have trouble explaining our disappearance."

Conniston said thickly, "Then get out. You're clear as long as you keep your mouth shut." His glance included Shannon, ominously. "One word of this, and you'll wish you had stayed lost."

Gil stood up, satisfied. "Let's go, Paul."

"Wait," Shannon said. "I've some explanations coming, first." He turned on Conniston. "This morning you used my identity to give a bogus interview to the visipress. I don't care that it cost me my job, but I want the truth about the rest of this thing. Who was the fat man who took my call to Gil, and how did the men he sent to stop me in Denver happen to have my suit and wallet?"

"Denver?" Conniston repeated. His heavy face went slack with astonishment. "Wallet? You fool, I never heard of you till this morning!"

Gil caught Shannon's arm urgently. "We'll have to look

62

deeper than Conniston to find the man behind that Denver business, Paul. This morning's interview was pure opportunism."

Shannon, sensing that Gil was right, went reluctantly. Conniston's surprise was too real to be false; too, he could hardly have been responsible for the web of inconsistencies that had been in the building since the moment Shannon landed at the Garrick farmhouse. Shannon left the apartment as much in the dark as ever.

The corridor lift dropped them smoothly to the lobby, but Gil did not go outside. He chose another cage instead that shot them upward again, this time to the roof.

On the landing, the night was clear and cool. The city lay below like a restless carpet woven of lighted streets and darker alleys, pulsing toward the center with a random beat of color that was like the pumping of a giant heart. Overhead, stars twinkled faintly, all but lost in the skyglow; the moon, rising, laid a smooth patina of light over the helicar that waited for them on the roof.

Shannon started when the machine's side port slid open and its pilot said urgently: "Get in. They're waiting for you on the street in surface cars, but Conniston may think to send a copter here any minute."

They were in the air before Shannon was seated. "This is Vince Harris, Paul," Gil said. "One of my research staff. A physicist, and a good one."

The pilot nodded and shot them, lightless, across the glow and darkness of Boston Metro. The helicar's cabin hummed to the purr of turbomotor exhaust and muted swish of blades, a sound too faint to drown out entirely the restless murmur of the city.

When they looked back from a distance, another copter was rising from the landing they had left, its searchlights stabbing the darkness in futile circles. Gil met Shannon's eye and grinned faintly when the searcher gave up the hunt and fell away.

"It's never safe to underestimate Conniston," he said. "He has his own tapecaster system in the apartment, of course, and we couldn't do less than assume that he'd have men waiting to follow us to our laboratory."

63

Harris, watching the copter's proximity scope, said: "All clear. Shall we go in now?"

"Take us down," Gil said. And to Shannon: "We're taking you to our own research center—not the one we set up to satisfy Conniston, though his money built it. You'll meet the rest of the staff there, and we'll fit you in."

Shannon was watching the city lights slipping past below like star-points on dark water, thinning and dimming as the helicar left the metropolitan area behind.

"That's the second time today I've been asked to join a world-saving crusade," he said. "I think I like the sound of your project better than Nugent's. At least you're making a fight of it."

Gil looked at him narrowly. "Is it really Nugent's project that rubs you wrong, or his daughter? She's one to linger in a man's mind."

"I hadn't thought of it," Shannon said. "But you may be right."

He sat quietly while the copter sank into darkness, sorting his thoughts and trying to assess them honestly. His memory of Ruth Nugent was disconcertingly vivid: the serious cant of her dark head while her father explained his project; her impatience with Shannon's refusal; the stricken look of her when she spoke of leaving her mother behind when the *Ark* blasted off.

He found himself comparing her with other women he had met since his return: the blonde stewardess on the stratoliner, the girl in the bar and, finally, with Ellen Keyne.

"You're right," he told Gil. "But it's resentment, not attraction. I keep thinking of the Nugent girl and Ellen at the same time, and it's an unfair comparison. Ellen was as attractive before she gave up waiting and went to that damned Sanctuary."

"You make a dubious point," Gil said. "Ruth didn't give up. She lost something, too, but she didn't go to the Cubes."

A block of dark warehouses slid beneath them, defined by empty, half-lighted streets. A roof rose to meet them; the machine settled, jarred and stopped. Harris opened the port and got out.

Gil took Shannon's arm. "End of the line. Let's get inside

64

while Vince garages the copter."

The building was an ancient hulk of concrete, relic of another day and time. They left Harris rolling the copter across the roof to shelter, and went down through a bulk-headed stairway into a glare of light and bustle of activity below.

The central section was like a huge three-storied hangar shaft, open from concrete floor to sheet-metal roof, a place loud with the clang of tools and bright with the flare of sodium floodlamps swung on traveling booms. In the center area, men in coveralls milled busily about two small bullet-shaped craft that stood in a minor forest of scaffolding. The ships were exactly similar, without jets and so unconventionally designed that Shannon could not guess whether they were intended for atmospheric flight or for space.

Other men in the laboratory worked at benches along the walls, wiring and testing electronic equipment largely unfamiliar to Shannon. In one corner the integration panel of a positronic calculator winked and flickered with complex patterns of colored lights, its sprawling bulk dominated by a small stooped man with mild, spectacled eyes and pointed, ermine-white beard.

Gil pointed out the operator with respect in his voice. "That's Miles Campion, perhaps the best space-stress mathematician alive. We were lucky that the Cubes didn't get him, and luckier to have him come in with us."

He identified four others, none distinguishable at a glance from the crew of bustling technicians.

"The staff." The pride in his voice denied his flippancy. "Five little heroes with their fingers in the dike, trying to save the world from its own stupidity. If the Cubist threat can be beaten, they're the ones to do it."

CHAPTER NINE

HE HAILED a red-haired young man in stained smock who came toward them, a metered test appliance in his hands. "Max Goff, Paul Shannon. Max, will you show Paul around? I've some progress reports to check."

With the tension of flight gone, weariness numbed Shannon like an opiate. In spite of himself he yawned before Gil had finished.

"Can the tour wait?" he asked. "I'm dead on my feet—I'd end the trip as ignorant as I started."

He yawned again and, annoyed, tried to recall when he had last slept. The memory startled him.

"My God, I haven't really slept for four days! I'll settle for a bunk now, and look your plant over later."

Gil laughed. "Take him up and put him to bed, Max, before we have to carry him up."

Max Goff gave Shannon a speculative look. "You're the one who spoke against the Cubes on visinews. Are you coming in with us?"

"The interview was a plant," Shannon said. "A dodge of Conniston's. Yes, I'd like to help Gil in any way I can—we've been friends since university days."

They went across the busy hangar to a freight elevator that slotted the wall. On their way they skirted the scaffolded ships, and Shannon felt a stir of interest in spite of his weariness.

"I never saw a design like that," he said curiously. "What are they, space or atmospheric?"

Goff laughed, pleased. "They're my babies until they're finished. We're going to need a couple of really fast spacecraft before this Cubist insanity is ended, so we're adapting Dace Nugent's stellar flight principle to power these two. Propulsion is gained through opposition of two conflicting gravitic curtains in a mass-magnetic field of—"

"Nugent's principle?" Shannon interrupted. They entered the freight lift and sent it upward. "The light-drive? I thought Nugent was keeping that quiet, that he didn't want it duplicated for fear of being followed some day by the wrong people."

Goff looked embarrassed.

"We don't like mixing espionage with research, but in this case we had to. We stole the idea from Nugent—couldn't let a thing like this be lost out around Procyon when we need it so desperately. Not that we're interested ourselves in stellar flight, but we can use it here inside the system."

66

An Earth Gone Mad

His face lighted with enthusiasm. He started to explain the basic facts related to light-drive. "When the time comes to put it to general use, it should revolutionize solar travel. It's far more efficient than atomics, and its limiting factor is just short of light-speed. These are two-man jobs; we've finished one already, except for provisioning, and the other should be ready within a few days."

They left the elevator for a bare corridor, and Shannon yawned again. Goff opened a door down the hallway and snapped on a light.

"Sleep as long as you like. You must really be bushed after what you've been through."

Left alone, Shannon sat on the edge of the bed and dug out his cigarettes, grimacing when he remembered that they were the same the stratoplane stewardess had given him on the flight from Denver to Boston Metro. He found it faintly incredible that only two had been consumed.

For some time he sat and considered the little package somberly, mulling over the things that had happened since it was given to him, but he never reached the point of lighting a cigarette.

He fell asleep first.

His dream was a thing of fantasy and cold terror, a queasy nightmare that left him shivering and sweating. It seemed that he was suspended high above a city whose every detail was microscopically clear in spite of distance, a place of great airy buildings and curving streets and green, spacious parks. People thronged the walks, the avenues flowed with bright, unhurried arteries. It was a city of peace and comfort and leisure, yet there was in the air of it a psychic abnormality that frightened him more than a physical threat.

For there was in the lines of every structure a skeletal suggestion of cubical articulation, an underlying alien motif in the architecture that brought him an alarm bordering on panic. And it seemed to him that the people in the streets moved too slowly and too closely in concert, as if they were the myriad feet of a hovering creature at once alien and invisible. Where there should have been haste, there was none.

67

The faces he saw, vanishingly small but impossibly clear, smiled without ceasing.

He sensed then that the people moved in a particular pattern, flowing together with an ordered precision that bore them along like chips on smooth-running water, never hurrying and never slackening. Bound together in some intangible fashion, they formed a whole that linked itself mysteriously with other wholes of other cities across the horizon. And beyond those . . .

He grew aware of another place coexistent with the city, not a part of it but superimposed upon it after the illogical fashion of nightmares: a desolate jumble of volcanic mountains among whose splintered crags rested a familiar domed figure, gray-green and brooding.

"You have lost touch with your world, Paul Shannon," the Kyril said. *"Do you wish now that you had remained on Io?"*

It studied him, and the city, with eyeless intensity. Shannon, beside it, saw that the people in the streets looked up toward him now without pausing in their course. Panic gripped him when he found every passing face familiar.

Ellen Keyne and her mother passed below, hand in hand, their tiny upturned faces smiling. After them came the stewardess of the stratoplane, and at her heels the two men who had met him at the Solar building in Denver; the man Fulmer, whom Shannon had run down on the highway at the Garricks', the girl from the bar who had gone to Metro Sanctuary—all following a spoke-like convergence of die-straight avenues toward a great Cube looming at the city's center.

After them all, a little apart, came a small fat man with pale eyes and carefully brushed gray hair, whom Shannon had seen on a radophone screen in Brighton. In his hands he carried a little square case that held the answer to everything.

The fat man, of them all, did not smile. He caught Shannon's eye from the distance and raised the case like one beginning a ritual, opening it—

Shannon woke, shaken to the roots of his sanity, to lie sweating and trembling until composure returned. He had found his discarded cigarettes and was smoking thoughtfully when the corridor door opened and Gil Lucas came in.

"I was beginning to wonder," Gil said, "if you were asleep or dead. I'm still not too sure."

Shannon got up and stretched, trying to put the dream out of mind. "I'm alive and starved."

Gil laughed. "You should be! You slept the clock around."

Thought of so much time lost disconcerted Shannon. "I wish you had called me earlier. I meant to see Ellen again, now that I'm over the first shock of what's happened. . . . Gil, I've got to find a way to bring Ellen out of that trance. Has it ever been done?"

"The Change is irreversible," Gil said. He took Shannon's elbow firmly. "We're at supper downstairs. Come on—we can talk about the Cubes later."

Shannon hesitated. The dream had so upset him that the memory of it lingered vividly in his mind, nagging at the fringes of his awareness with a disturbing suggestion of significance overlooked. It could not be more than an exhaustion-induced nightmare, but so many improbable things had happened to him that he could not dismiss it easily.

"I had a dream," he said, "that frightened me more than the lava-lions frightened me on Io. Do you mind if I tell you about it?"

Gil looked at him oddly when he had finished.

"I don't wonder you're upset—this whole thing, if it comes to that, is more like a nightmare than fact. No, I don't think it means anything, except that you've been under too great a strain."

He frowned faintly. "You must have seen a visinews flash of it or heard someone describe it, for there really is such a place. Ohio Peace Center, the Cubist training site not far from Toledo."

"I hope I never see the place at first hand," Shannon said. He felt a dampness on his forehead at the prospect. "Gil, it wasn't *right*. It wasn't like a city at all—it was more like a living organism of some sort, a composite creature beyond human ability to understand. I can't find the words—"

"It was a dream," Gil said. "Forget it."

69

He clapped Shannon on the shoulder. "Let's go downstairs before those gluttonous techs strip the tables."

As soon as he had finished eating his old urgency settled on him like a weight. He crushed out his cigarette and stood up. "Have you a radophone, Gil? I want to call Ellen."

"In my office," Gil said. "Second door to your right down the corridor, just past the first-aid room. But don't set up our identity code when you call, will you? We're on a masked circuit here, and can't afford to have it traced."

CHAPTER TEN

THE RADOPHONE was a standard unit that responded normally in spite of the illegal circuits that kept it from exchange notice. The Keyne residence code flickered across its screen under Shannon's touch, blanking out at once when the call was taken.

His uneasiness mounted sharply when he saw that it was Myra Keyne who answered.

"Where is Ellen?" he demanded.

Her answer stunned him.

"The Servants transferred her to Ohio Peace Center this afternoon for assignment. I wish you had called earlier, Paul. Ellen would have liked seeing you before she went."

"Transferred?" he echoed dumbly. "Assignment?"

For the moment, his mind refused the idea; when he accepted it, he could think of nothing but the Garricks and their own assignment, dying at the hands of Normal murderers to set peace as a reality before the world.

His dream came back to him, and with it a cold certainty of disaster. He saw Ellen's upturned face, smiling and tiny, and felt again that she was being moved along a course inexorably set for her.

"A Mr. Nugent called for you earlier," Myra Keyne said. "He hoped to find you here, and was disappointed when I couldn't tell him where you were. He asked that you call him . . ."

She broke off. "Wait, Paul. Someone is at the door."

An Earth Gone Mad

"Don't answer it!" Shannon said sharply. "Stay where you are. I'm coming over!"

He ran without waiting to clear the circuit, through echoing corridors and across the cluttered hangar room and up the bulkheaded stairway to the roof. The helicopter that had brought him there waited, empty and dark, under its concealing shed.

He rolled it outside and wrenched open the port. Within seconds he was in the air, spearing through the night toward Boston Suburban.

The Keyne neighborhood was not hard to find from the air, but the inevitable small delays of locating key arterial avenues chafed Shannon's patience unbearably. When he found the right intersection he came down out of the night recklessly, disregarding the flutter of aerial traffic, and set the copter down heavily on the Keyne lawn.

The wrecked surface car in the driveway told him that he was already too late.

The machine leaned drunkenly against one corner of the brick porch, a crumpled heap of scorched and twisted metal. A thin trickle of leaking fuel tinkled on the driveway underneath it, loud and pungent in the evening stillness.

Shannon cut his own motor and ran up the steps to the house. The living room was empty, the hallway dimly lighted and silent except for a faint clicking sound. He moved toward it, and caught himself up just in time to avoid stumbling over Myra Keyne's body. She lay unmoving in a small, quiet heap, her gray Cubist gown torn and disarranged, her dead face serene and utterly content.

The clicking resolved itself from the hallway shadows. Shannon, moving in, saw Ruth Nugent at the radophone unit, fingers busy with a half-completed calling code on the screen.

"*You*," Shannon said. "What are you doing here? Who did this?"

She turned a strained face to him, her eyes dark and enormous with shock. She had exchanged the brown coveralls for evening wear, a full-length white dress cut low at the shoulders under a short, dark jacket with huge iridescent buttons. The change in her was startling; she seemed softer,

71

more feminine and somehow less imperious.

"I came here to find you," she said. The fright went out of her voice and her chin tilted. "My father called this afternoon and missed you. Tonight he sent me."

She came toward him, leaving her calling code unfinished. At closer range he saw that her hair was disarranged and that her jacket was torn, disclosing an ugly bruise on the bare shoulder beneath.

She drew back a little at sight of Myra Keyne's body. "Zimmer Conniston's men did that—don't ask me why. I recognized one of them; we had trouble with the Guild when we first opened our shops to build the *Ark,* and this man was one of their agents. They—"

He cut her short, impatiently. "You're wasting time. Start at the beginning, will you?"

The whine of a siren approaching outside, shrill and incisive, prevented further talk.

"Civil patrol," Shannon said. "We'd better get out of this. Come on, I've got a copter outside."

He lifted them from the lawn seconds before the lights of a patrol car swept the house. There was a confused flashing of searchlights below and a single pale shock-ray stabbed upward, but none touched their speeding helicar.

"The Guild men were there when I came, a few minutes ago," Ruth said. "Their copter was on the lawn. . .   They came out of the house, running, and opened fire on my car. They used an exploder, or something else heavier than a hand weapon, and smashed it. I think I must have been unconscious for a few minutes from the shock. When I went in, I found . . . what you saw. I can't imagine why they should have killed poor Mrs. Keyne."

"Because she had seen them," Shannon said. "I should have expected something like this, after meeting Conniston. He sent them for Ellen."

"For your fiancee? Why?"

"To shut my mouth—and through me, to keep Gil Lucas quiet. Thank God the Servants reached her first. She's safer with them than with a crew like Conniston's."

"The Cubists came for her? I don't understand."

"They took her to Ohio Peace Center for assignment,"

72

An Earth Gone Mad

Shannon said. When she would have spoken again, he cut her off brusquely: "Quiet. I want to think."

The glowing disk of Boston Metro drew near, expanding against the dark earth. Shannon slowed the helicar and turned it back toward Suburban, choosing a course that would circle the outskirts while he tried to make a choice from alternatives left.

"Your father sent you to find me," he said finally. "Why?"

"Because he felt that by now you must have learned how useless it is to fight the Cubes," she said. "And because he still wants you on the *Ark*."

She made a small sound of disgust. "Alec and I were taking an evening off for dinner and a play, but Father broke it up with an emergency call to the theater. Father is afraid we'll have to advance the *Ark*'s takeoff date. Our plant is picketed already--the *Ark* isn't safe there any longer, and neither are we."

"Picketed?"

"Not by the Guild--by Solar Service musclers. Solar has fought us from the beginning because Father opposed the spread of Cubism."

The girl touched his arm, her eyes following the serpentine tangle of lighted streets below. "There's the plant, over there. Drop to the right, or you'll miss it."

Shannon laughed shortly. "I'm not heading for your plant. I'm going to Ohio Center after Ellen."

When she stiffened in sudden alarm he added sourly, "Don't get excited, you're safe enough. I haven't time to take you home, but I'll put you down at a shuttle terminal on the way."

She stifled her anger with an obvious effort. "Please, Shannon--Solar may move in on us before morning. I've got to get back to Father."

"And to Alec Blair," Shannon said. He regretted the words instantly.

"Alec and I expect to be married once the *Ark* is under way," she said. He felt her speculative glance in the gloom of the copter cabin. "Why shouldn't I be with him when trouble comes?"

Shannon shrugged. "It's nothing to me. .   I'll set you

73

down at your plant, on second thought, for an equal favor. Is the *Ark* armed?"

"We've a store of small arms, but not enough to equip the whole staff. Government restrictions on sale of weapons prevented that. Why?"

"Conniston may send men to Peace Center for Ellen," Shannon said. "If they arrive ahead of me, I can expect trouble. I'll need a dart-gun or exploder—preferably a dart-gun, since it's smaller."

She looked at him curiously. "You're a strange man, Shannon. You can't bear being beaten, can you?"

"Your father asked me to join him for that reason," Shannon pointed out. "There's a law of survival I never guessed at until I cracked up on Io—if something blocks your way, smash it. The lava-lions taught me how effective it can be. And how final."

She fell silent, her eyes on the lights below.

"All right," she said presently. "I'll get a weapon for you if you'll take me home. It's nothing to me if you and Conniston's musclers murder each other."

He sent the helicar down in a steep curve toward the dark huddle of shop buildings, aiming for the faint sheen of light reflected from the *Ark*'s polished hull. They were almost above the barbed fence that guarded the plant grounds when the entire area lighted up suddenly with a harsh flare of sodium floodlamps.

Shannon fought the controls, half blinded, driving the copter back into concealing darkness.

Below them he glimpsed tiny figures running like ants from the shop buildings, converging upon the towering bulk of the *Ark*. Lights came on in the ship, outlining every opening; more tiny figures leaned from personnel ports, helping the running men inside.

Other hurrying shadows came out of the night beyond the fence, gathering in a tight knot before the gate. Two of them carried something between them; they halted and a swift, thin streak of violet fire arced up, passed close by the *Ark* and exploded with a searing white flash against a shop building.

The building vanished, raining a hail of fiery debris. One

of the running figures staggered and fell within its own length from the ship. The rush of air from the blast reached Shannon's copter, sweeping it high on a thunderous shock-wave of concussion.

He righted the machine in time to see the wounded man drawn inside by his fellows. The ports snapped shut. The coppery length of the *Ark* glowed a sudden, sullen red—

It went up swiftly, the reaction of its thrust crushing the shop buildings below like cardboard houses. A howling wind swept the area, gathering dust and debris and tumbling the men outside the fence like twigs.

Far up at the limit of vision the speeding red dot of the ship turned a brilliant, electric blue—and vanished.

"The light-drive," Ruth Nugent said in a choked voice. "They made it. No one will overtake them now!"

A helicar streaked out of the darkness, circled the broken shop buildings and settled to disgorge a packed body of armed, running men. Another followed, swinging wide in landing to clear the first.

Shannon turned his own machine at full throttle, driving low to avoid being silhouetted against the sky, and streaked back into the night. He looked back several times, but so far as he could discover there was no pursuit.

"We're back where we started," Shannon said. "You've missed your ship, and I'm no nearer to Peace Center."

Ruth sat quietly, considering. "I don't know what to do. Father will send for me when it's safe—but how can I let him know where to find me? And I'll *have* to hide. Solar wouldn't hesitate to kidnap any one of us and drag the *Ark's* base location out of us with *hypnol.*"

Metro drew beneath them again, and its nearness posed again the need for decision. Shannon let the helicar hover, suspended on a faint sighing of blades, while he tried to sort out the difficulties ahead. Some would be normally innocuous little encounters made dangerous because of his unfamiliarity with the new changes. He had been on Earth only two days; how much was there that he did not know yet, but which Ruth Nugent would know as a matter of course?

"You mentioned a base for the *Ark*," he said. "And that

75

An Earth Gone Mad

means that she's still inside the solar system somewhere. Where?"

She looked at him sharply, weighing her answer.

"You may as well know, since we seem to be in this together. She'll be on Io, taking on crew and supplies. We never kept more than a construction gang here to finish and test the ship—the rest have been waiting there while we stockpiled for the flight."

He stared at her, thunderstruck. "Io? You've had a base there all the time?"

"For something over a year, since we first began the Ark."

The realization that other men had been on Io during the greater part of his ordeal shook him impotently.

"My God, I needn't have lost that last year at all," he said. "I could have worked my way around to your base and got back in time to stop Ellen before she gave me up for lost!"

It occurred to him then that the Kyril must have known about the Nugent base, and he wondered why it had kept the knowledge to itself. The immediate answer was too obvious to miss—it had wanted to keep him on Io. Why? For the first time he doubted the Kyril, and, remembering the cryptic good-bye it had given him, he wondered with a fresh uneasiness if it might not itself be a part of the plot against him.

He dropped the thought as worse than useless. "Your father can't help you from Io. We'll have to make our own plans."

She answered him indirectly, out of her own concerns. "You must have found someone here to help you, else you wouldn't have a helicar tonight. Why can't we go to them?"

He realized then the predicament into which his headlong impatience had thrown him, and cursed himself bitterly.

"We can't find them. I took the copter on the spur of the moment after I called the Keyne house and found Ellen gone, and I don't know the way back. I don't even know Gil's radophone code."

He felt the incredulity of her glance and laughed shortly. "Go ahead and say it. I'm a fool, and I'm lost."

76

CHAPTER ELEVEN

HE COULD not afford to delay long.

"It needn't matter," he said. "Even if I found Gil I'd go on to Peace Center."

"Unarmed, against Conniston's musclers?"

He had already dismissed his lack of weapon as irremediable. "I'll worry about that later. The problem is what to do with you."

"That's no problem," she said instantly. "Since I can't stay here, I'll have to go with you. But I'll keep the bargain we made, a weapon for my passage."

He weighed her assurance against his own ignorance and found the offer tempting.

"I don't know. . . . Having you to look after would offset the advantage of being armed, even if you found a gun."

She laughed, the first real amusement he had seen in her. "We've each an enemy to run from, Shannon—suppose I threatened to warn Conniston that you're going to Peace Center?"

He stared at her. "You'd do that if I left you behind?"

She could not resist prodding him. "Remember your Ionian law of survival, Shannon! It works as well for me as for you."

He laughed in turn, his resentment going. "There's that. But what's to prevent my dumping you out here and now, to keep you quiet?"

"I wondered if you'd think of that. But you wouldn't do it."

He sobered. "Of course not. I'm no murderer."

"And I'm no informer."

"It's a bargain, then. Find a gun for me, and I'll keep you out of Solar's way."

He puzzled over her certainty while he dropped the helicar toward the city below. He could, and would, destroy anything that blocked his way to Ellen, but he knew without examining his reasons that he would not have harmed

77

this girl. He disagreed as violently as before with her defeatism in giving up humanity as a lost cause; he was obscurely affronted by her assurance in the face of his own ignorance, but these were side issues that did not bear on his acceptance of her.

In the end he was surprised to find a certain comfort in her presence. At least he was no longer alone.

"Put us down here," Ruth said suddenly. "We can't use any of the regular Metro landings. There's sure to be a patrol warning out for us by now, but they won't look for us in the dock section or at Ansel's place."

The helicar dropped into the first darting fringe of metropolitan traffic. Commercial aircraft droned by, using the higher lanes for speed; a Suburban shuttle lanced past with a giddy blurring of ports, red proximity lamps blinking from its wingtips. Shannon snapped on the copter's riding lights, feeling that a darkened machine would be more conspicuous here than a lighted one, and chose a descending lane.

The restless dark mirror of the bay rose under them, pinpointed with a glitter of bobbing lights.

"Guild territory," Shannon said. "A rough neighborhood, after dark. . . . Who is this Ansel?"

"A contrabander," Ruth answered. "Government hasn't stopped the sale of weapons, it's only driven the traffic out of sight. When Solar spiked our application for Government arms we went underground for them, to Ansel, though they cost double the market price."

They circled the wharves twice to find a landing place away from the termitic bustle of the piers.

Below them great rusty tankers nosed at moorings, decks shining greasily in the floodlight glare. Cranes swung loads of barrels and bales and boxes; men and machines scurried endlessly, like ants fleeing a violated nest. Tiny patrol boats skittered like water beetles from ship to shore, searchlights stabbing officious fingers into every business.

They found a deserted pier and put the helicar down in the shadow of a warehouse. With the opening of the port the damp, fishy smell of the bay closed in upon them, heavy with the odor of oil and exhaust fumes and rotting refuse from the fruit boats.

An Earth Gone Mad

An empty barge bobbed below the pier, waiting for cargo. Its crew clustered about a foaming deck-trough, naked bodies glistening under the harbor lights while they washed their gray clothing. They sang as they worked, a calm, slow harmony that contrasted sharply with the hard alertness of guards watching from lookout posts.

"Cubists," Ruth said.

Her voice shook a little, and it came to Shannon that the singing men had made her afraid as she had not been afraid even in the Keyne house. "Content wherever they are, like cattle. And there are more every day. We'll all be like that some day, Shannon, unless we get away in time."

They left the helicar for an alley-mouth that led up to the waterfront streets above.

"We'll find a way to stop them," Shannon said, "without running."

In the alley they were conscious of each other only as shadows in a confusion of shadows. Now and then a random wash of light from the bay searchlights touched the warehouse walls on either side, lighting their way palely. For the brief moment they could see the broken pavement underfoot, and avoid the stinking miscellany of garbage that littered it; when the glow was gone the darkness rushed back thicker than before, forcing Shannon to draw a hand along the cold face of the building to keep his way.

They moved on without speaking. The end of the alley lightened slowly.

"Turn here," Ruth said when their alley intersected a wider street. "Ansel's pledge-shop is only a little way from the docks, else I'd never have come here."

Two blocks brought them to a dingy shop that huddled, dimly lighted and uninviting, beside a brawling casino. They went in hurriedly to avoid the drunken crowd milling in and out of the pleasure house, and blinked in musty gloom until their eyes adjusted.

Dusty glass cases tiered the walls, displaying an improbable miscellany of pledged valuables: gold-handled knives, wrist chronos, precision kits of tools, wigs and ornaments, delicate silver jewelry and oddly glazed pottery looted from the ruins of Martian cities and pawned here for the price of

An Earth Gone Mad

a drink. Shannon was examining the stuff, fascinated by its variety, when Ruth touched his arm.

"Let me do the bargaining," she whispered. "They mustn't know that we're here on our own, without Father behind us."

To the man who came toward them from the back of the room she said, "You'll remember me, Ansel—Miss Nugent. We've taken on a new recruit, and need another dart-gun."

"I remember you," Ansel said. He was a heavy man, middle-aged and bald, with a square, sullen face and pale eyes that considered the girl with sly interest. "I wouldn't forget one like you."

He jerked a finger toward the back of the shop. "This way. For a price I'll get you any kind of weapon you want."

They followed him into a smaller room full of light and smoke and the stale stink of alcohol. The place was empty except for a man and woman who sat at a bare table, the man small and expensively dressed, the woman young and hard with a practiced, metallic hardness. Both were intent on a private diversion, their laughter bursting harshly on the air like the discordant barking of dogs.

On the table between them something wavered unsteadily on tiny splayed feet, its ten-inch body already bloated with the beginning of Terrestrial decay, a dirty glass clutched in one three-fingered hand and a smoldering cigar in the other. Shannon recognized it at once—a Titanian native, the only quasi-intelligent life men had found in the solar system and a species so close to extinction that exportation from the Saturnian moon had become a penal offense.

It bobbed its acorn of head at Shannon, its snouted little face hideous with moronic exultation. *"More men,"* it gobbled. *"I am men too, see?"*

The woman laughed shrilly. The man splashed whiskey into the creature's glass. "Then drink like men. Get drunk!"

It drank. It staggered on aimless feet, drooling, searing itself with the cigar, its idiot ego wholly engrossed in the business of aping humanity.

Shannon turned away to see Ansel grinning at him, patently enjoying his reaction.

80

"It's dying on its feet," Shannon said. Anger made him sharp.

Ansel shrugged. "It's their pet." Suddenly he moved across the room to a radophone unit recessed into a wall niche. The screen lighted at his touch; when Shannon moved toward him in sudden suspicion, the shopkeeper raised a hand in signal to the little man at the table.

"Hold him, Chiro," Ansel said. "This is the man Guild listed for pickup. Conniston wants him."

The man at the table took a dart-gun from a jacket pocket and turned it on Shannon. Neither he nor the woman spoke. In the sudden silence the little Titanian stumbled drunkenly on the table, gobbling memorized obscenities.

Conniston's face appeared on the screen, cigar in his mouth. His scowl froze at sight of Shannon.

"I don't want you any longer, Shannon," Conniston said instantly. "I want Lucas. Where is he?"

Shannon shook his head. "I don't know."

Conniston studied him warily, and even through the flat monochrome of the image the tension that drove the man was plain. The bloodshot weariness of the Guild leader's eyes told Shannon a part of the answer—Conniston had not slept, which meant that he was facing an emergency too great for temporizing.

Conniston tried again.

"I made a mistake when I threw Lucas out," he said. "I need him. I need him so badly that I may lose this fight against the Cubes without him. *Where is he?*"

"I don't know," Shannon said.

Ansel took a step forward. "Let me handle him, Mr. Conniston. Chiro and me—"

Conniston silenced him impatiently. "Hold him there until I send for him. And be careful—he's not important, but he's dangerous."

Behind Shannon the little Titanian giggled senselessly; there was a sudden scraping of chairs, and the woman screamed angrily. He turned to see her scrubbing furiously with a handkerchief at her coat, which the creature had just fouled. Chiro cursed shrilly and struck the Titanian with

81

his fist, smashing it from the table to a corner where it lay whimpering and retching.

Shannon went in instantly, too fast for Ansel's startled bellow to mend the break. Chiro's arm was thin and impotent in his grip; he wrenched the dart-gun from the man's hand and flung him after the Titanian, turning with the same movement to face Ansel.

Ansel had a weapon half out of his jacket pocket, his pale eyes starting with his effort at haste. Shannon shot him before the gun was clear, the dull concussion of explosion shaking the room like the dropping of a heavy weight.

Chiro lay unmoving, his feet almost touching the writhing Titanian. The woman had backed against the wall, her face pallid under its cosmetic smear; Shannon considered her coldly, and his regard made her terror a strain too great to bear. She fainted across Chiro in an angular, graceless huddle.

Shannon went toward them, ignoring Ruth's frozen cry: "Shannon—Paul, please!"

He stepped across the unconscious pair to the corner where the Titanian lay moaning and struggling to rise. Its legs flopped grotesquely under its broken back; its discolored eyes looked up at him piteously, and something in their uncomprehending agony reminded Shannon forcibly of the girl he had met in the bar.

"*Men,*" it croaked. "*See, I am men . . .*"

"You might have been," Shannon said dully. "Some day, if men had let you alone."

He stood back, sick with sudden revulsion, and ended its whimperings with the dart-gun.

Ruth's cry brought him up short. The radophone screen had gone blank; a rumble of voices from the street and the immediate crashing-in of the pledge-shop's front door told him that Conniston had used his time to good advantage.

"The back way," Ruth was calling. "There's an alley there, if they haven't blocked it—"

They went out into darkness loud with the clamor of men pouring from the casino next door. This time they did not feel their way, but ran blindly with a single thought between them: to get back to their helicar on the docks.

CHAPTER TWELVE

THE ALLEY led into another street, a wider way that ran at
right angles to the one on which the pledge-shop faced.
They followed it for a block at top speed before the
sound of pursuit reached them, and took another alley to
the left when the glare of hand torches stabbed the darkness behind them. They came out of the second alley to
the heavy smell of the waterfront, and at the end of the
first down-sloping block they picked out their landing pier
by the sound of Cubist voices singing from the barge.

The helicar stood where they had left it, a deeper shadow
in the lee of the warehouse. They crouched beside it, looking sharply for pursuit, but no one was in sight.

In the helicar, it was Ruth who took the controls. Shannon slumped beside her, surrendering to an overpowering
lassitude that drained him of purpose. There was no need
now to drive himself. . . .

The reaction passed finally. He sat up shakily and tapped
a cigarette alight, passed it to Ruth and lit another for
himself.

He watched a city-glow slide past on the horizon, and
fished with the copter's communicator for its identity. The
microwave beam came in strongly from an unseen stratoport, mechanical voice placing their location with monotonous precision: "*Albany, New York. Weather fair, visibility
unlimited to Syracuse, Scranton, Reading. . . Low-ceiling
rain west of Rochester, Pittsburgh. Time, 2319. Albany,
New York . .*"

"We're making fair time," he said. "We should reach
Toledo by morning."

She looked at him in surprise. "Toledo? Peace Center
isn't there—it's well to the east, between Fremont and Sandusky Bay."

She laughed in genuine mirth that eased the restraint
between them. "You *do* need help. You were all set to
descend on Conniston's crew, alone and unarmed, and you

83

didn't even know where you were going! Suppose you had left me in Metro? You'd have set down in Toledo, asked the wrong questions and been arrested on the spot!"

He laughed with her, ruefully. "Another wrong conclusion. There's a lot more I don't know, too. But I've only been back two days, remember."

"Then you might as well tell me what you do know," Ruth suggested, "and let me fill in the blanks. Why not start with Io?"

Shannon shut off the communicator and told her everything. The relief he felt in sharing his frustration was, oddly, as satisfying as it was unexpected.

When he had finished, they were well past Youngstown to the south, entering the rain promised by the Albany microbeam. Ruth had given the controls over to the autopilot to listen; she sat half facing Shannon, her eyes wide and dark in the faint wash of light from the instrument panel.

"But it's so *pointless*," she said. "Though the things that have happened to you couldn't possibly be coincidence or error. . . . But if your part in them was planned, they'd have had to know when you'd land, and where—and that means they'd have known you were on Io from the beginning, and that our depot was there, too!"

"The question," Shannon said, "is *who?* Either Solar or the Guild, if they knew about your base, would have moved to stop you by now, I think. And who would be interested in chivvying me about like a trained seal?"

"It's too subtle for Conniston," Ruth said. "And it's even less likely that Solar would have kept the information so long without using it. They'd have ruined us long ago."

Shannon yawned, lulled to drowsiness by the monotonous beat of rain against the helicar's hull.

"That leaves the Cubes," he offered. "There's a sort of insane method in the routine I was put through, an outlandish logic that fits their peace-through-submission campaign to absorb Mankind."

She was silent, and he went on: "What do the damned things want of us, really? Why are they here? The threat of extrasolar invasion has been dinned into us, from one

84

source or another, since the first interplanetary flight—but who'd have thought it could come like this?"

"The pattern they've followed—" Ruth began.

"That's the word for it," Shannon cut in. A chill of excitement made his scalp prickle. "There's a pattern behind all this, a sort of alien blueprint for conquest that makes no sense to us because it wasn't drawn up by our kind of intelligence. And whatever shaped that pattern is very, very sure of itself."

He shifted restlessly in his seat, tapped another cigarette alight and returned the pack to his pocket when Ruth refused one. Unexpectedly, the mood that had fallen upon him in talking to the girl in the bar came back, leaving him depressed and bitter again.

She took the controls back from the autopilot and said coldly, "I'll be as happy as you to have this fool's errand over with. I'm only anxious to get back to my father and Alec."

The sudden return of coolness between them left Shannon disproportionately irritated.

"You should have stuck with them instead of waylaying me at the Keyne house, then. Neither of us would be here now if your father had kept to his own affairs and let mine alone."

In the stiff silence that followed, an ironic possibility passed through Shannon's head. He voiced it, baiting her with deliberate malice.

"Your father wanted me aboard the *Ark* badly enough to offer me command of colonization. Had it occurred to you that he might need me enough to strike a different sort of bargain for my services?"

She looked up from the controls, puzzled. "I don't know what you're driving at."

"He'd have to offer compensation," Shannon said. "I'd be leaving everything behind and starting alone again. And two years of being marooned on Io convinced me I wasn't meant to be a bachelor."

"We considered that in choosing the *Ark*'s crew," she said. "Three-fourths of the personnel are women; you'd have no trouble finding a wife or companion. That's the purpose of a colonizing expedition, to populate new worlds."

He laughed at the color that rushed to her face when she realized what he was driving at.

"Suppose I traded my services for the privilege of choosing my own woman, and picked you? Would your altruistic urge to save humanity balk at that?"

She said scornfully, "I'd stay behind on Earth first!"

Shannon settled himself more comfortably in his corner of the seat. "Don't worry, it won't come to that. *I'm* staying."

She turned to watch the rain streaks that patterned the port glass, ignoring him. Chuckling, Shannon fell asleep.

He woke to find that the helicar was no longer airborne and that he was alone. The rain had stopped. It was hot and close in the copter cabin, and the silence was like a weight.

He opened the port and climbed stiffly out, feeling for the dart-gun in his pocket, and found himself standing ankle-deep in wet grass. The sky was still dark except for a fat white moon silvering the cloud-banked western horizon and for a lesser glow that filtered through the trees to the north.

The glow was very close. When his eyes adjusted to the near-darkness, he estimated that the building from which it came lay less than a hundred yards away.

He went toward it cautiously, holding the dart-gun ready because he did not know what he might find. The dew-wet undergrowth drenched his clothing and left him shivering. The wind on his face was cool, heavy with the night-smell of greenery and touched faintly with a smell of turbomotor exhaust fumes.

The highway before him came as a complete surprise.

It lay pale and ribbon-straight between the trees, vanishing to north and south in the gloom. He wondered briefly where it led, knowing that stratoliner service and copter-freighting had all but replaced inter-city traffic, and came to the conclusion that Ruth must have chosen a place near a major center of population to abandon him.

Her desertion puzzled Shannon. He could have understood her leaving him in Boston Metro. Why leave him here?

86

An Earth Gone Mad

He was still mulling over this latest inconsistency when a white glare of sodium lamps blazed up on the highway ahead and the whine of a turbomotor came to him. He moved hastily back from the roadway and crouched in the undergrowth, waiting to see what came.

The vehicle was not a private surface car, as he had expected, but an antiquated passenger bus that rattled and fouled the night with poorly burning fuel vapors. Its interior was lighted by a scattering of overhead bulbs, the illumination barely strong enough to show him what passengers it carried.

Except for the driver, they were all Cubists.

The bus slid past and was gone toward the south. Another followed; Shannon, looking closely, saw that its passengers too were Cubists.

The third vehicle was not a bus but a truck, topless and railed about the edges. It was loaded to capacity with more Cubists who stood shoulder to shoulder, as tireless and serene as placid gray statues.

Shannon did not linger to see the rest of the convoy.

He went back the way he had come, swearing under his breath when he stumbled in the darkness. All the Cubists in the country, he thought, must be on the move, if this were a sample—but why, and to what place? The converts recruited by Servants of the Cubes must run to an enormous figure daily, but not so many as to require convoys to deliver them to Peace Center.

Peace Center.

The thought that he might be so near startled him. A Cubist train could hardly be bound for any other place—but why move at night, and in such numbers?

His speculation brought an answer more disturbing than before. A general hegira of Cubists from the cities to Peace Center could mean only one thing: the dissension that had built for so long was drawing to a head, the jarring factions were coming to grips and the Cubists were fleeing to Peace Center for protection.

And that, in turn—

Someone came out of the darkness, calling his name softly. He put the dart-gun away in quick relief when he

87

recognized Ruth Nugent.

"*Shannon!*" she said. There was a sharp edge of panic in her voice. "Shannon, is that you?"

"I thought you had deserted me," he said. "Where are we?"

She made a small sound of relief. "For a moment I was afraid it wasn't you, after all. . . . We're between Fremont and Sandusky Bay, just north of Ohio Peace Center."

In the helicar again, Ruth placed a plastiwrapped parcel of sandwiches on the seat between them. "There's a roadhouse of sorts back there for surface commuters. I thought we'd better eat before we go on to Peace Center."

He did not touch the package at once. "You went back there all alone in the dark, knowing you might be picked up? You must have been starving, to take a risk like that!"

"As a matter of fact, I'm not hungry at all," she said. She unwrapped the package and opened a steaming bottle of coffee. "I had dinner with Alec before Father sent me to the Keyne house. A very good dinner, the sort I'm not likely to have again soon."

Her composure, as usual, rubbed him wrong. That he should benefit from her voluntary risk annoyed him still further.

"Then you brought these for me. Putting the barbarian in his place, is that it?"

CHAPTER THIRTEEN

LATER, SHANNON said: "You must have been at the roadhouse for some time. Did you see the Cubist convoy?"

She crumpled the empty sandwich wrapping and tossed it outside. "It was reloading when I stopped there. They'd had a meal before going on to Peace Center."

"I thought Normals wouldn't serve them under any conditions."

"It's a Cubist holding now," she said. "Though it's open to any traveler. . . . They wouldn't take money for my sandwiches, did I tell you? It seems they don't use money among themselves."

88

She took the cigarette Shannon offered her and looked at him searchingly over its glow.

"Are you sure you want to go through with this, Shannon? I'm afraid Ellen Keyne will be safer at Peace Center for the next few days than outside. There's going to be open trouble everywhere—the convoy of Cubists was running away from it."

"I guessed that," Shannon said. "Conniston must be taking his first step against the Cubes, and Orsham's moving to stop him. Gil was right—it's going to be a bloody business."

He shifted impatiently. "But I've got to get Ellen out of that place. If Conniston and his Guild go all out, they may attack there."

"The Center is under Government protection," she reminded him. "The military took over weeks ago, and they've prepared against any sort of demonstration. The syndicates forced the move, of course, but that's beside the point—an open attack will be too risky even for Conniston unless a general uprising of the Guilds draws away enough troops to make it practical."

He admitted the soundness of her argument but saw that saying so would leave him at loose ends again, his mission still unfinished. The longer he considered the choice the greater his restlessness grew, and with it his urgent need of finding Ellen.

"I've got to go," he said bluntly. "Can we scout the place first without being shot down?"

"We can try," she said, and slid the port shut.

They took the machine up in the first graying of dawn, and Shannon saw at once that they were nearer to Peace Center than he had thought. In the dark open country below them sprawled a wide crescent of lights, its twinkling cusps lying on the southern horizon; when they drew nearer, the sickle extended itself to a full half-circle and then to an ellipse that ringed in the Center.

"The post lights of Government troops," Ruth said.

The size of the installation dismayed Shannon. He had expected a token guard, a minimum cordon thrown up to satisfy Government's obligation. But to find the Center ringed with barracks and drill-grounds and stratofighter fields was something else again.

The Center, formless in the early fog and darkness, took shape and pattern with the dawn. A soft glow outlined the overall arrangement, discovering a concentric series of broad curving streets that lapped outward to intersect die-straight avenues converging to a central building like spokes to a hub. Shannon, assessing the capacity of the place with an engineer's eye, estimated a minimum population of half a million.

"They're stronger than I guessed," he said. "No wonder Conniston is frantic! With three Centers like this in the States, and at least one other in every major country, it's only a matter of time until the Guilds are drained completely."

The sun came up with a burst of red light that touched the taller buildings of the Center, glinting on glass and metal and polished stone to set up black, angular shadows that threw the underlying architectural motif into bold relief. A sense of familiarity grew on Shannon, rousing an uneasy premonition that set the short hair to prickling on his neck.

He had seen that same inconsonant motif in his dream, its odd architectonic stylization peering through stone and metal like the outlandish tracery of an alien skeleton.

His disquiet mounted when he followed the convergence of avenues to the central structure and found it a key to the whole. It was manifestly an administration building, square and featureless—like a gigantic Cube.

Finer details appeared as the helicar circled: gray-clad Cubists moved in the streets, soldiers in pale blue uniforms poured out of barracks and marched briskly to mess halls. There was a general scurrying of messengers and official vehicles.

"We'd better land," Ruth said, "before we're challenged. They're probably tracking us already and wondering what we want."

Shannon pointed. "I think that's our spot of entry, out there beyond the guarded area where the Cubists are coming in."

90

An Earth Gone Mad

The fields beyond the bivouac area were jammed with an improbable jumble of vehicles: trucks, turbobuses, helicars and cabin planes, all of them dark and empty. A commercial air shuttle arrived while they watched, settling near the northern gateway to disgorge a slow swarm of Cubists.

The swarm became a column that joined other columns moving in through the gate. Perspiring guards passed them in like cattle, making room for those who pressed behind. A sort of ordered confusion prevailed, a resistless bustle that should be next to impossible to check accurately.

"Set us down in the field just beyond the gate," Shannon directed. "I'll go in on foot from there."

Ruth dropped the helicar at a steep slant into the jumble of grounded craft. A second shuttle settled almost beside them and began discharging a cargo of smiling Cubists.

"You won't get through in Normal clothing," Ruth said.

He nodded, engrossed in the scene before them. "I don't expect to."

He moved out, keeping the helicar between himself and the guards at the gate. A Cubist passed within arm's reach, and Shannon blocked his way. The man stood quietly, smiling, without hint of surprise or impatience.

"Take off your clothes," Shannon ordered.

Obediently, the man stripped off jacket and trousers and stood in underclothing as drab and rough as his outer garments. Shannon slipped the commandeered clothing over his own and turned back to Ruth in the copter. She nodded with an expression halfway between disgust and admiration.

"You'll pass," she said, "except for your face. What can you do about that fierce black scowl of yours, Shannon?"

"I'll get by," he said.

He lingered, reluctant now to break the unsuspected bond that had grown up between them. "Don't wait for me. I've dragged you through too many risks already. Take the copter and hide until you can get in touch with your father."

"And if you don't find Ellen?"

He shrugged. "I don't expect to fail."

She copied his shrug, mocking him. "I'll wait. Partly because you'd never get back to Boston Metro without me, and partly because I'm anxious to see you stride out of

91

Peace Center with your fiancee slung over your shoulder like a Sabine captive. There's nothing so refreshing as honest stupidity."

He turned away, his face burning, and fell into the line of Cubists moving toward the gate. At the entrance he tried to smooth his angry face into something of Cubist serenity, and felt a sinking sense of inadequacy when he realized that Ruth had been right—he could put on Cubist clothing, but not the Cubist look.

Luck and the sweating weariness of the guards passed him through. He was inside Peace Center and lost in the scattering gray flood before sounds of disturbance at the gate told him that the Cubist he had stripped had been halted for questioning.

The slow press of bodies bore him without incident into the streets of the Center proper. There he found himself even more at a loss than he had anticipated; the gray people went their ways with bee-like certainty, and he was left alone.

At close hand the regularity of arrangement confused him badly. He followed the ever-narrowing block segments for a time toward the center, but found every curving street the same, every radial avenue duplicating identically the one he had just left.

The buildings were largely dormitories, with here and there a basic-service establishment: leather shops and markets, laundries, commissaries supplying linens and cafeterias serving steady streams of newly arrived Cubists.

There were no wine shops or tobacco stores, no offices or exchanges or other businesses indispensable to Normal living. And nowhere did he find any evidence of money changing hands. The city operated functionally, without haste or waste or bargaining, and in that busy hive Shannon was utterly lost. He was alone in a place designed to hold five hundred thousand persons, a shining alien place without signs or guides, and he did not know which way to turn.

And the Center grew more crowded by the minute.

In the distance Shannon could hear the sound of arriving and departing vehicles, the hiss of passenger shuttles and whine of overloaded copters—and still they came. For the first time the real enormity of what he had undertaken came to him, and he marveled at the ignorance that had let him think he might find Ellen here.

It had all been for nothing, then. He had endured two years of hell, and had come four hundred million miles; he had survived threats and frustration and attempts on every hand to hamper him, and he had forced his way finally here to find defeat.

For a moment the futility of it made him almost ill. He was worse off now than before, for when he left Ruth Nugent with the copter he had given up his one reassuring contact with normality. Ruth would be on her way back to Metro now, bending her whole attention to the problem of getting word to her father and Alec Blair.

The little park he stumbled upon then was as welcome as an oasis to a desert traveler: a quiet retreat of close-cropped grass and graveled walks winding through thickets of shrubbery, the whole shaded to coolness by a scattering of tall trees. There was a fountain, and a pool, and occasional white benches.

He turned into the place as into a sanctuary. He had drunk from the fountain and was washing face and hands when the sound of his name froze him with shock.

"Mr. Shannon! Then you *did* go to the Sanctuary after all!"

He whirled, feeling for the dart-gun in his pocket, and saw that it was the girl he had met in the Metro bar.

She was exactly as he had last glimpsed her in the green gloom of the Metro Sanctuary, all the hurt and bitterness gone out of her eyes and the awkward defiance vanished from her grave, childish bearing. Her eyes widened at Shannon's look, but her smile did not waver.

"No, you didn't see the Cube," she said. "Or you'd have changed as I have. I am sorry for you, Mr. Shannon."

The shoe, he thought dully, was on the wrong foot now. In Metro, he had been sorry for her.

"You're wearing Cubist clothing," she went on. "Why?"

"I had to get in," he answered. "I came to find my fiancee."

She shook her head wonderingly. "In all this? Peace Cen-

93

ter is a big place. I'm afraid you've had your trip for nothing."

Her glance moved past Shannon and stopped, turning him.

A big man in tattered Normal clothing shambled out of the shrubbery toward him, muttering incoherencies, bearded and filthy and gross with a dissolute heaviness of face and body. In the early sunshine his mouth glistened wetly, and his eyes had a fixity of stare that suggested less than sanity.

He carried an arm-thick section of broken tree-branch, a ragged club already stained and battered with use.

"*Parasite,*" he said thickly, and swung at Shannon's head.

Shannon staggered back, too stunned to do more than avoid the blow, and would have fallen if the Cubist girl had not put out a hand to steady him. The bearded man moved in swiftly, grunting; Shannon pushed the girl away and ripped open the Cubist blouse that covered his street clothing, digging frantically for the dart-gun in his jacket pocket beneath.

The weapon caught in the coarse fabric of the blouse and spun away to fall beyond reach in the grass by the fountain.

The club's upswing was like movement in a nightmare, frozen to impossible slowness. The Cubist girl stood to one side without moving to run or to interfere, her face serene and untroubled.

Someone in Cubist gray darted out of the undergrowth, caught up Shannon's fallen weapon and fired in a single continuous motion. The bearded man went down heavily under the explosive impact and lay, grotesquely broken and twisted, on the grass. The fountain from which Shannon had drunk a moment before tinkled musically, loud and careless in the sudden silence.

Ruth Nugent stood with the weapon hanging slackly in her hand, swaying uncertainly. Her face, turned away from the man on the ground, was white and strained against the shapeless gray of her Cubist clothing.

Shannon said in numb disbelief, "Ruth! How in God's name did you get here?"

"I followed you," she said. Exasperation lightened the

94

shock in her eyes. "You utter fool, did you think I'd let you leave me behind?"

He took the dart-gun from her and turned it over absently in his hands, searching for words. "I never expected to see you again."

He saw then that the Cubist girl was still there, interested but totally unaffected by what had happened.

"You'd better go," Shannon said. "There's no point in your being involved in this."

"It doesn't matter," she answered. She moved away, smiling. "Don't worry about it. The Bearers would have sent a Cube for him soon, anyway."

She disappeared along the graveled path, leaving Shannon and Ruth alone. Ruth began to cry quietly, and the sound drew him guiltily to her.

He took her arm and led her away, past the fountain and the thing on the grass. "You've had trouble enough on my account. Let's get out of this madhouse."

She went willingly, but once on the path she posed the question that had troubled him most. "You're going to leave Peace Center without Ellen?"

"I don't know," he said helplessly. "For the first time, I'm at a dead end. . . . Ruth, what shall I do?"

She shook off his hand and the plea with it. "I can't tell you that. The decision isn't mine to make."

They rounded a curve in the pathway and halted at sight of the man who sat on a white bench at the turn. A small, old man in neatly conservative street clothing, who raised a thin and scholarly face at their approach and studied them disinterestedly with light, weary eyes.

"I heard the shot," he said. "That would have been the end of Dr. Calder, I think."

CHAPTER FOURTEEN

"It's quite all right," he said when Shannon stared. "He was quite mad, and homicidal. The Bearers would have come for him soon in any case."

An Earth Gone Mad

He chuckled without humor at their bewilderment. "Your assailant was Dr. Lawrence Calder, until recently my colleague in a field investigation of Cubism at its source. Our study succeeded too well, as you can see."

Recalling the other's filth and idiot ferocity, Shannon found the title oddly incongruous. "*Doctor Calder?*"

"Once a neuropsych specialist like myself, and later a parasite on the bounty of the new order," the old man said. "I am Professor David Latimer, if it matters."

They took a bench across the walk from Latimer and sat down, facing him.

"You're the first person I've met who really seems to know anything about the Cubes," Shannon said. "What did you mean by *Bearer* and *parasite?*"

"The Bearers," Latimer told him wearily, "are the Cubes' special agents, sent when occasion demands to convert a Normal who causes them too much inconvenience. Calder's insanity, and his club, made him a minor irritant—a Bearer would certainly have brought a Cube soon to stop him. Parasites? Calder was one, as I am still. . . . There are hundreds of Normals in Peace Center, most of them criminal degenerates and neurotics who take what they like and do as they please. They lack the courage to make the Change, but are equally afraid of returning to Normal life and to the police. Most go as Calder went, eventually. The Bearers come for the rest."

"I didn't know the Cubes used force," Shannon said. "I thought their gospel was one of peace."

"The end justifies the means," Latimer said. "The Cubes will inherit the planet sooner than anyone thinks—their Bearers filter through society everywhere as Normals, speeding up the conversion at key points. I might have made some attempt to warn the world, but it was too late already when I came here. Mankind is doomed, young man. Make no mistake there."

Shannon moved uncomfortably, recalling an identical statement Dace Nugent made two days before. Two days? The lapse surprised him—it had seemed weeks.

"For the first time," Latimer said, "humanity has met with something entirely beyond its ability to understand. It
96

may be better so. Too exact a knowledge of the Cubes might be worse than the Change itself, their Plan too alien to be grasped with sanity."

Gil Lucas had said: ". . . *so wild that even a telemovie fantasy show wouldn't touch it."*

For a moment, Shannon felt that he was about to learn at last what Gil had meant, and the thought left him suddenly indecisive, torn between an eagerness to know and a dread of knowing.

"You know what the Cubes are and what they're doing to us," he said. "Will you tell us?"

Latimer shook his head.

"Why should I? You would go as mad as Calder and take the knowledge with you, or give up hope as I have and become a parasite on the new order. You would stretch out your empty existence here, ashamed to live and afraid to die, going your way like a dead man while you waited for a Bearer to come with a Cube and claim you altogether."

He stood up, his thin face flushed.

"I am a parasite, on a level with the stupid beetles that creep into termite burrows and live on the sufferance of their hosts. I am going to the Center now for breakfast—a Cubist will feed me, another will wash my clothing or clean my shoes or do whatever I ask. I may have anything I require until the trifling nuisance I represent brings attention and a Bearer.

"You are still free, and you have nothing to gain by learning more than I have told you. Get out of Peace Center. Get away from Earth, if you can. Make the most of your time—it will not be long."

He moved away, walking with an erect dignity totally at variance with the despair he had voiced. Shannon and Ruth watched him out of sight before either spoke.

"Poor devil," Ruth said. She shivered, her annoyance with Shannon forgotten. "Paul, do you think he was right about the Cubes?"

Shannon shook himself, trying to dispel his depression.

"I think he's crazier than Calder was." He stood up, admitting defeat on one hand and taking up new purpose on the other. "You were more right, I think. It's going to take either an organized fight or open flight to beat them, and if I can't find Ellen here I may as well go back to Metro and do what I can to help Gil. Let's go, shall we?"

The military encampment was fully astir when they made their way back from Peace Center to the encircling bivouac area.

Shannon and Ruth halted just inside the gate, watching the gray tide in dismay. The swarm of entrants was even greater than it had been at dawn, and was still growing. There was no counter outgoing current; it had been easy enough to enter Peace Center unnoticed, but he saw that getting out would be another matter.

Ruth saw the difficulty as well. "Paul, what are we going to do?" ·

The bivouac was surrounded by barbed entanglements, patrolled and impenetrable. They might have risked stealing a helicar from the military motor pools inside, but Shannon knew without considering the odds that they would never take it out. Stratofighters waited on their fields, jets warmed and ready; from half a dozen latticed towers the parabolic reflectors of proximity-warning beams swiveled, alert for any aerial movement.

"We'll have to go out the way we came in," Shannon said. "Through the gate."

He saw Ruth brace herself for the ordeal, and knew that she was remembering Latimer's warning of what would happen if they stayed.

"Then let's go," Ruth said, and pushed her way into the steady flood of Cubists pouring in from the gate.

A dozen yards from the entrance, the incoming press became all but solid, parting reluctantly as they worked their way forward. It was desperately slow going; Shannon saw before they were well begun that the commotion of their contrary passage must certainly draw the attention of the gate guards.

The guard had been doubled since morning. Three blue-clad soldiers stood at either side of the gateway, shock-rods ready, scanning the incoming crowd with harried impatience. Beyond them the Cubist flow converged from the cluttered landing area to file in a solid column toward Peace Center.

Over their heads Shannon could see the wild jumble of abandoned craft that had brought them; he even picked out his own helicar, sitting a little apart from the others beside an empty shuttle. Another copter rested just behind it, but it was not deserted—its pilot stood in the open port in an attitude of searching, his short body bent to peer intently toward the gate.

They were within arm's reach of the gate when the guards discovered them. A blue-uniformed figure came toward them through the crowd, shoving forcibly at placid Cubists.

"You two—stop where you are. No one goes out!"

Other guards followed, closing in. The Cubist column, momentarily blocked, packed closer and bulged outward, breaking its ordered ranks. Shannon took Ruth's arm, lowered his head and bored into the milling mass.

There was a confusion of shouts and flickering shock-rays. A Cubist went down beside Shannon and was trampled underfoot. A guard fell. Shannon felt an unexpected slackening of pressure before him and found that the press, miraculously, had opened to let them through.

Two guards were down, ringed by Cubists who held their ground patiently to avoid trampling them. Another stood rigidly in the gray mass, closed eyes and set pallor telling Shannon that a shock-ray had touched him. The other three came unheedingly through the break, shock-rods glowing.

The pale finger of a ray from outside the melee touched them, and the way was clear.

Outside in the open, Shannon drew Ruth toward the helicar. Someone sprang down from the high-rounded top of a passenger shuttle at the gate and ran beside them, panting.

Shannon brought up his dart-gun defensively, and almost dropped it when he saw that the man beside him was Gil Lucas.

Shannon's copter was nearest. They piled into it, breathless, and Shannon lifted the machine at a steep slant, throttle wide. Gil crouched behind him, calling urgent orders.

"Keep low, or they'll have us on their scopes. Head for the trees there to the north—we can run for it in them if they force us down."

His order was too late.

Pursuit ships rose from the bivouac fields behind them, circling like swift flights of birds to hem them in. From one of them a sleek, egg-shaped interceptor missile darted out, jockeyed on robot jets and whipped toward the helicar in sharp, warning bursts.

The ultimatum was too plain to mistake.

"They've got us," Gil said. "Set the copter down, Paul, or they'll blow us to dust."

Shannon let the copter settle, obediently preceding the circling interceptor that herded them back toward Peace Center. Beside him Ruth sat quietly, eyes watching Shannon with an odd blending of fear and pity. Gil squatted on the floor beside the port, following the darting of the missile outside.

When they touched inside the bivouac area, Ruth put a hesitant hand on Shannon's arm. "Be careful, Paul. Please— they'll kill you if you resist!"

Shannon got out without answering her. Gil and Ruth followed, Gil holding Ruth's arm to steady her.

"Throw your gun away," Gil said. "You can't fight your way out of this! Do you want Miss Nugent killed, too?"

"No," Shannon said dully. "I don't want that."

He tossed the weapon back into the helicar, feeling a cold conviction of guilt at the possibility.

"I'm sorry I brought you into this," he told Ruth. "I should have known I couldn't fight a thing as big as this."

She smiled at him fully for the first time, and the fright went out of her eyes.

"We'll find a way out," she said.

The robot missile overhead darted back to its parent ship; the stratofighters wheeled in formation and returned to their landings. Armed men came running across the drill fields, blue uniforms shimmering in the sunlight.

A patrol squad took over, headed by a blond young captain with a clipped mustache and an air of icy efficiency.

"You are trespassers in an area restricted by Government

order," the captain said sharply. "Come with me."

He did not speak again, or allow speech among his prisoners, until he had released them into provost custody at the encampment prison.

"Your disposition rests with the post commander," he said, before leaving them. "Colonel Tichnor will see you soon."

Their cell was like the rest of the camp, without comfort but serving the function for which it was designed. Two bunks, two chairs and a table made up the furniture, all bolted securely to the floor. The walls were of flinty pressed-plastic, broken at one end of the room by a barred window and at the other by a barred door. From the hallway outside an armed guard watched them, his look bored and disinterested.

Shannon fought down the impulse to pace like a caged animal and sat down on one of the bunks. Gil sat on the other, smoking and watching Shannon curiously.

"How did you find us?" Shannon asked. Another thought rose to puzzle him, and he frowned at its obscure similarity to other and older facets of the same riddle. "And how did you manage to be at the gate just when we made our break?"

"You left the Keynes' calling code on my radophone," Gil reminded him. "When you didn't come back, Max Goff and I made an undercover check, and when we learned that Myra Keyne had been murdered and Ellen transferred to Peace Center, we took it for granted that you'd come here. It was typical of you."

He offered Ruth a cigarette, and when she refused he passed his case to Shannon. Shannon accepted and sat holding the little cylinder absently without lighting it.

"I couldn't know when you'd try to leave Peace Center," Gil said. "I found your copter and waited, knowing you'd need it once you realized what you were up against here. I was about to give you up when I saw you coming out."

Shannon lit his cigarette and stood up restlessly. A gleam of reflected sunlight caught his eye from outside and he went to the window to scowl across the dusty sweep of drill grounds toward the shining glass-and-stone expanse of Peace Center.

"How long will they hold us here?" he asked. "And what will they do with us?"

"They won't keep us long," Gil said, "else they'd have separated us. I think we'll be taken before the post commander at once, but what happens after that will probably depend on whose long arm reaches us first."

"Orsham and Conniston will want us when they know about our arrest. Is that what you mean?"

"And Government. Don't forget that illegal entry into a restricted military zone makes us spies," Gil said. "Also the civil police have you on list for complicity in Myra Keyne's death, for the killing of that pledge-shop owner, and for possessing a contraband weapon."

He grinned wryly when Shannon turned on him. "Oh, I'm in the same boat! Government has a pickup order on me as a subversive, plotting against Cubism in defiance of the official tolerance order. Conniston should share the charge, since he hired my research staff, but that's beside the point. Conniston swings enough weight to escape it. I don't."

Shannon went back to his window.

"Conniston must have started his push against the Cubes," he said, "or there wouldn't be this rush to Peace Center. Has there been any actual violence yet, Gil?"

Gil turned sober. "No bombs dropped yet, but the break is due any moment. Conniston has been gathering his muscle-squads for days, getting ready for the drive. When it comes—"

He got up and stood beside Shannon, rising on his toes to see outside.

"Conniston knows now what he should have understood months ago, I think. He's going to lose this fight, Paul, but he's too pigheaded to admit it. The Cubist Change is going to wreck the labor empire he's built, whether he fights it or not, and he's working on the idea that he can't lose more than that by making an all-out stand.

"He'll use all the force he can muster. He's already dropped any pretense of negotiating, and he doesn't care any more about such minor matters as keeping you quiet. He doesn't want Ellen any more to control you, so you can stop worrying about her falling into his hands. He only

102

wants me now, because he can't do without me."

Shannon, watching the Cubist horde pouring through the northern gate, found a hint of confusion in their ranks. The long gray column wavered while he watched, fell back and split to make room for a speeding line of turbomotor surface cars.

Every car was paneled and windowless, painted with a pattern of brilliant red-and-white stripes designed to make it visible for instant identification.

"Hospital cars," Gil said. "It's come sooner than I thought."

CHAPTER FIFTEEN

FOR WHAT seemed hours they watched the hospital convoys racing through the gate, until the last car had gone and the gray column closed again. Red-and-white planes began to appear in the bivouac area, filling drill fields and post streets to disgorge gray figures that carried others on stretchers.

"Strange, isn't it," Gil said, "that Cubists won't evade individual attack, but will run from a threat to themselves as a body? I think their running to Government now means the beginning of the end, Paul, because this attack of Conniston's will bring trouble such as the world never saw before. Humanity has survived a million plagues and three atomic wars, but it won't survive this. When it's over, there'll be nothing left but Cubists."

His certainty was appalling. "You'd like to know how it will happen? The Guild will go all out to destroy the Cubes, and the syndicates will move together to prevent. Government will rush in, forced by pressure from both sides—there won't be any neutrals. Everybody will fight but the Cubists, all over the world. The fighting will spread everywhere, and when it's over only the Cubes and their following will be left."

Ruth came to stand between them and watch the patient gray tide. "But they look so calm and helpless! It doesn't seem possible that they could win."

103

An Earth Gone Mad

"Divide and conquer," Gil said. "The little people never want to fight—wars are won with their blood, and they don't like dying. The Cubes are taking advantage of that; when this trouble is bad enough, they'll draw the little people into their Sanctuaries and their troubles will be over. So will the world's."

Shannon turned on him almost angrily.

"You're talking like the old lunatic we met in the park, who knew all the answers but wouldn't tell. How do *you* know all this, Gil?"

"You'll see it too, in time," Gil said. "Remember what I told you that first night in Conniston's apartment, about the Change's being too fantastic for—"

He was interrupted by a four-man guard detail, led by the same blond young captain who had brought them to their cell.

"Colonel Tichnor is ready to see you," the captain said.

They went on foot to headquarters, through an orderly confusion of military activity. Work details passed, loaded with tools; turbotractors whined by, dragging loaded caissons. On the drill fields soldiers marched and swung and pivoted, weapons winking through the dust of their marching.

The colonel waited for them behind a bare expanse of desk, a squat gray man with cold intolerant eyes in a fat-creased face, his body gross and heavy in its overtailored uniform. Years of command had lent him an arrogant dignity that reflected itself sharply in the frozen respect of his subordinates, but to Shannon's dreary perception he was only another minor atom of deluded ego, impotently stranded on the hummock of his own identity.

A civilian stood beside the colonel's desk. It did not surprise Shannon to see that it was Clayton, the Solar personnel superintendent who had paid him at Orsham's order in Boston Metro. Ironically, it occurred to Shannon that he still carried Orsham's draft in his wallet and that it would never be cashed.

"These are the three," Clayton said. "You'll find Solar eager to prove her gratitude for your cooperation. Will you provide an escort to return the girl to Boston Metro?"

104

An Earth Gone Mad

The colonel drummed on his desk top, austerely pleased with himself. "And the other two?"

Clayton shrugged. "We need the girl to negotiate an understanding with her father. The others are of no consequence."

He looked at Shannon vindictively. "You should have retracted that interview, Shannon. There's no profit in fighting Solar."

"They'll give you no further trouble," the colonel said. "I have full emergency authority here." He caught the blond captain's eye: "Arrange an escort for the girl. Execute these two."

The captain snapped to attention. "Detail—"

"No," someone said from the doorway. "The plan has changed."

Recognizing the two men at the door was to Shannon like a completion of the cycle of unreality that had begun three endless days before. They were the same who had intercepted him at the Solar building in Denver and put him aboard the stratoliner.

They had promised him then that his questions would be answered in due time, but now they ignored him as if he did not exist.

"We are here," one of them said, "by personal order of President Orsham, to take charge of the prisoners."

The colonel looked questioningly at Clayton. Clayton scowled uncertainly. "I recognize you as members of the president's staff," he said reluctantly. "But this—you have a written order for the transfer?"

"There was no time," the man said. "Don't delay us, please."

Suspicion flared in Clayton's eyes. "I don't believe you! Colonel, will you order these men held until I can radophone Solar for instructions? I think they are—"

"You think we are Guild agents," the man said. "And your suspicion will force us to act against our will. Has it occurred to you that we might be Cubists instead?"

Clayton said contemptuously, "They can't be Cubists, Colonel. Arrest them."

The colonel frowned speculatively, and Shannon could

read the weighing of probabilities that went on in the man's mind. Solar owed him a reward for his services, and he had no intention of risking it.

"A radophone call is soon made," the colonel said. "You'll find a unit in the cabinet behind you, Mr. Clayton."

The two at the doorway moved apart, and a third man came between them into the room. He was a small, fat man with sparse gray hair carefully brushed to cover an incipient bald spot and pale eyes that considered those in the room with impersonal deliberation. In his hands he carried a little black box. That held the answer to everything.

Sight of it turned Shannon back to the sweating fantasy of his dream. He moved back instinctively, drawing Ruth with him. The colonel stood up behind his desk, his fat face angry. The blond captain fidgeted uneasily, waiting for orders; his guards moved together behind him, like children huddling for reassurance. Clayton gaped palely.

"You're no Solar operative," Clayton said. "Nor a Guild agent. *Who are you?*"

"A Bearer," the fat man said, and raised the box like one beginning a ritual. "Bringing you a Cube, and peace."

To Shannon and Ruth he said sharply: "Turn your backs!"

When they turned, he opened the box.

The Cube floated between his hands, a coruscant block of soft green light that warmed the room to its deepest corner, radiating a serenity that was like the aura Shannon had felt at the doors of the Metro Sanctuary, but subtly different and infinitely stronger.

The silence was like death.

To Shannon it seemed that he drifted in warm euphoria toward a place of indescribable content, a haven of peace beyond the definition of peace. He was only conscious of Ruth beside him; her hand in his was like a touch in a dream, but singularly pleasant because it meant that he would not be alone in the drowsy paradise toward which he floated.

He never reached it. Sight returned first and then sound. Sunlight caught his eyes from the polished surface of the colonel's desk; he heard a distant clanking of tanks and caissons, blurred by distance, and the far, soft rhythm of marching men. Somewhere a bird sang, full-throated and blithe. Shannon shook himself at the sound of footsteps leaving the room.

The colonel still stood behind his desk, but the arrogance of him had given way to a serenity that glowed like an intangible extension of his being. The captain and his guards stood tranquilly, none similar in face or build but all alike as wax dolls poured from the same smiling mold. Cubists.

The Bearer had gone, and with him one of the two who had come with him. The other waited briefly in the doorway to speak to Shannon.

"We did not lie to you in Denver," he said.

Shannon would have followed, but Gil caught his arm. "Don't be a fool, Paul—we've got to get out of here!"

Escaping Peace Center now was so easy that it was hard to believe they had ever been in danger. The colonel himself escorted them to their helicar and stood smiling while they boarded it. The blond captain and his detail waited placidly with him, weapons discarded and no faintest trace of military stiffness in their bearing. Clayton they had left at the office, serene as a bald Buddha in street clothing.

At the last moment, Shannon paused to look back at the shining pile of Peace Center.

"My fiancee was transferred here yesterday from Boston Suburban," he told the colonel. "Is it possible to find her in that?"

The colonel shook his head regretfully. "I'm afraid not. Peace Center keeps no individual records, and in a press so great . . and tomorrow there will be millions."

"I thought not," Shannon said.

Still it took time to grasp the finality of it. He could only leave Ellen there, giving her up, after coming so close.

He sat blindly in the helicar beside Ruth while Gil lifted the machine and turned it eastward. Ruth put a hesitant hand on his arm and he shook it off with unconscious roughness, unaware in his depression of her concern.

They passed over the fields beyond the litter of abandoned Cubist vehicles and entered open country. For a time the air was thick about them with copters and shuttles bringing more refugees, and once they paralleled for a while the highway which Shannon had stumbled upon the night before, a pale ribbon still acrawl with Cubist-laden cars.

CHAPTER SIXTEEN

THE STRAINED silence of the copter cabin jarred on him finally and he roused to find Ruth crying softly, without sound.

"What is it?" he demanded. "What's the matter?"

She did not answer and he put a hand under her chin and tilted her face so that he could see. Her eyes were dark and enormous and glistened with tears; her mouth quivered, attempting resolution and failing.

"I know it's stupid of me," she said. "But all at once I couldn't bear seeing you beaten after what you've been through."

Shannon stared at her in amazement. "My God, you're sorry for me, after what I've dragged *you* through?"

Gil passed his handkerchief to Ruth and looked at Shannon in exasperation. "Let her alone, will you?"

Shannon turned on him sharply.

"Then we'll talk about something I've puzzled over since you first found us at Peace Center. A little truth from you might explain some of the insanity I've been tangled in from the night I came back to Earth."

He settled on the most immediate of a long list of discrepancies. "You've admitted knowing a lot more than you've told about all this, Gil. That affair in the colonel's office— why did the Bearer warn us to turn our backs? Why didn't he take Ruth and me along with the others?"

Gil shrugged patiently. "I've been expecting that. Can't you take the Bearer's word for it that you're not ready to know?"

He looked to Ruth for support, and found her watching him with a share of Shannon's speculation in her eyes.

"You, too?" Gil said in half-bitter amusement. "Why should it matter to you, when you're planning to leave it all behind the moment you can get back to the *Ark?*"

He turned back to Shannon. "Why ask me?"

108

"Because you know what is behind it," Shannon said. "I'm not accusing you of being a part of it, but I think you're keeping back something that affects Ruth and me directly. . . . Why did the Bearer refuse us?"

"Because you don't fit their pattern," Gil said patiently. "Remember what the Servant told you at Metro Sanctuary, that you were not acceptable? Don't ask me why! But someone has gone to a staggering amount of trouble to guide your movements—has it occurred to you that whoever pulls the strings in this puppet show has a part for you in it important enough to justify his trouble?"

"I can't imagine what it would be," Shannon said. "Gil, you once said you were afraid to follow up your premonition about the Cubes too closely for fear it might be right. You know definitely now what they are, don't you?"

Gil nodded reluctantly, his round face strained.

"I think so. It's a tremendous thing, and so fantastically simple that you'd never believe me unless I showed you proof. And I can't show proof now. We've got to get under cover first."

"We're going into hiding?" Ruth asked.

"You didn't think Government would drop charges against us, did you? We're still fugitives—the fact that the colonel turned us loose doesn't change that. Another officer will be in charge by now, and he'll want to know what became of us. It won't take him long to find out."

He clicked on the helicar's proximity scope and made a quick horizon check. No pursuing pip appeared on the screen, and he shut the instrument off.

"The air is clear," he said, "but not for long. Government isn't the only power after us—either Solar or the Guild would jump at the chance of getting rid of us. Orsham is as determined to stop the *Ark* as Conniston is to get hold of me, and catching Ruth would give him his chance."

Mention of the *Ark* brought Ruth back to her own problem with a start. "I'd forgotten that! Father will be trying to find me, and someone may be able to trace him back to our base on—"

Shannon cut her off sharply. "Shut up! Do you want to give the *Ark* away?"

When she stared at him in astonishment he said, "I've just realized what it was that happened in the colonel's office that struck me so wrong. The Bearer warned you and me to turn our backs, Ruth. *But he didn't warn Gil.*"

She put a hand to her mouth and looked at Gil in horror. He gave her his wry, square-toothed grin and she shrank back against Shannon.

"You think I'm a Cubist agent like those who came with the Bearer," Gil said. "I can't blame you for being suspicious, for how can you be sure of what I am? For that matter, how do you know that Ruth here isn't a Cubist in disguise, too?"

"I don't," Shannon said. "I've no way of knowing anything."

Another possibility even more disquieting came to him, laying his corrosive uncertainty in the open. "How can I tell what either of you really are? I may be a Cubist myself without knowing it."

There was a silence while they stared at each other in uneasy speculation.

"There you have it," Gil said presently. "We're on even terms now with the rest of the world. No one knows whether his neighbor is Normal or Cubist, and there's no way of finding out until it's too late. But we'll get nowhere accusing each other—why don't we let the question wait until we're safe in Metro?"

"I wish I could forget it altogether," Shannon said slowly. "We've been friends a long time, Gil. But I've got to know the truth about this."

"You won't wait till we reach my lab, where I can explain it properly?"

Ruth said suddenly, "Paul and I can't be Cubists, even unknowingly."

She was still pale, but when Gil turned on her she met his look levelly.

"How?" Gil demanded.

"Because Cubists don't kill, even the Bearers. And Paul and I have both—"

She broke off, and Shannon knew that she was remembering the blasted thing they had left by the fountain in the
110

Peace Center park. He put a hand on hers, reassuringly. "Don't think about that. It's done with."

Gil shrugged round shoulders. "The best defense is a good offense, especially in the hands of a woman."

He reached into his jacket and brought out the dart-gun that Shannon had tossed into the helicar before their arrest at Peace Center. "That should make you feel safer. Relax, will you?"

Shannon weighed the weapon thoughtfully in his hand. "I suppose I should be properly shamed, but I'm not. I still want to know, Gil."

Gil made a helpless sound and clicked on the copter's scope again, watching it narrowly while its slender green finger explored the horizon.

"It's not a thing to be explained on the run," he said, and touched the proximity indicator. "We're going to need all our wits and attention to get away at all."

He took the helicar down steeply. A small river rose to meet them, placid water gleaming like silver between screening trees. Shannon, checking the scope, saw a tiny pip winking at its western edge, moving swiftly across the gridded disk toward the central hub that marked the copter's position.

"A stratofighter scout," Gil said. "Searching for us. We'll have to trust to luck that it hasn't spotted us."

He set the helicar down on the river bank between sheltering trees and cut the turbomotor. The breeze that came in when he opened the port had the fresh smell of approaching evening, a sound of running water and the calling of birds invisible in foliage.

"This is as good a time as any," Shannon said. "We may not get back to Metro at all, and I've got to know about this. There's still Ellen, remember?"

"I won't attempt to explain it offhand," Gil said stubbornly. "The theme is simple, but the allied basics—do either of you know anything about the operation of the human subconscious? How it reacts in obedience to instinct and stimuli to control the body independently of the conscious ego? Do you know how hormone action maintains systemic balance among cells?"

111

His sudden earnestness left them floundering.

"No one really understands those things," Shannon said. "I think they're passed over in our education for lack of facts, like the old mystery of collective intelligence among termites. But I'm not interested in biology, Gil. I want to know about the Cubes."

Gil said wearily, "And I refuse to discuss them. It's not the reasoning that's obscure, entirely; the idea itself is too fantastically simple for belief on one hand and too damaging to the ego on the other."

He checked the proximity scope for the speeding strato-fighter pip, and found it gone. "It'll come back," he said. "Or another will. We'd better wait."

They chafed under the strain of mutual distrust until the pip appeared again on the eastern rim of the scope, returning. The Sun had gone down behind the trees by the time the plane disappeared from the screen, and the cool gloom of evening moved across the river to hide the glint of running water from them.

They waited for another hour before Gil lifted the copter, dark except for its faint glow of panel-bulbs, and turned it north.

"We're not far from Cleveland," he said. "We'll be safer above the lakes, where we can keep low enough to dodge proximity scopes without risking our necks over uneven terrain."

A few minutes later he dropped the helicar low over Lake Erie and drove through the darkness so close above the water that they could hear the soft wash of waves above the turbomotor whine. Shannon got no more from him; he balked argument by refusing to speak until the subject was dropped.

Shannon gave it up finally and lapsed into sullen silence, mulling over the little he had learned. Ruth, tiring of the impasse, switched on the copter's visiscreen unit and fished among the commercial channels for newscasts.

News was plentiful, but so slanted by partisan delivery that it was next to impossible to reach the truth of what had happened. Syndicate stations gave accounts of Sanctuary bombings, of mass attacks on Cubists and wholesale sabotage of properties by Guild muscle squads. Guild stations countered with claims of industrial provocation, stressing near-bloodless worker's-party victories.

Government bulletins stated tersely that the situation was under control, that public rioting was being quelled by military and civilian corps and the public could expect quiet within a matter of hours.

"Lies," Gil said wearily. "Do you wonder we're losing? Even now it's more important to justify our own stands than to compromise and fight together. I think the race has managed to exist this long only because it never faced an enemy stronger than its own greed."

The visiscreen blared on.

> . . *Cubist menace of world proportions, heroic drive by Guild forces to rid our beloved Earth of her alien invaders.* . . *Argentine Peace Center bombed, Puerto Rican Sanctuaries leveled by howling worker-mobs* . . *estimated slaughter in Chicago reaches staggering total of one hundred thousand already* . . ."

"For God's sake, shut it off," Shannon said finally. "If we don't know what to believe, there's no point in listening!"

They flew on into the night. They skirted the skyglow of Rochester and dropped to skim across Lake Ontario, the soft whine of turbomotor and lapping of water blending into a drowsy monotony. Shannon felt Ruth relax against him, and saw when he looked down that she had fallen asleep.

Sound and motion were infinitely comforting; before he realized it, sleep overtook Shannon as well. At one moment he was listening to the interminable splashing of water below . .

The next, shaken from sleep by an abrupt change of course, he was flashing low above the lighted expanse of a city.

113

CHAPTER SEVENTEEN

GIL TURNED a dim face toward him in the darkness.

"We'll be at my lab in a few minutes," he said, "if I can shake the police craft that just picked us up."

The pursuing helicar was not dangerously close but hung on doggedly, search-beam stabbing the darkness in the swift rush of aerial traffic. Shannon, watching from the rear port, knew precisely how the other's proximity scope must look—spotted and streaked with the flashing tracks of legitimate craft until trailing a single unlighted machine through the confusion was like pursuing a particular bee through a swarm.

"They challenged me just inside Metro limits," Gil said. "Government must have alerted every civil patrol in the country for us."

A Suburban shuttle overtook them on the right, ports checkering the sleek curve of its rushing bulk. Gil raced the helicar alongside it, ignoring its flurry of proximity warnings. On the patrol craft's scope the two pips would be merged to one; in the crush of traffic it would be next to impossible to know when the smaller detached itself.

"There's the lab area," Gil said. "See if they follow us down."

They dropped into a canyoned labyrinth of warehouses. Shannon, craning his neck upward, saw the patrol ship flash past overhead.

"We're clear," he said.

The jar of landing woke Ruth. She sat up, yawning, and stifled the yawn when she caught the familiar city-glow about them.

"Boston Metro!" she said. "We're back already?"

"It's 0400," Gil said. "You've slept for hours."

To Shannon he said, "They'll have to search the whole area to find us now, and I think they're too busy for that."

They waited on the graveled landing while Gil stowed

114

the helicar away. On the dark stairway below, Ruth kept a light hand on Shannon's shoulder to guide her. The sound of their passage echoed ahead and behind; when they stopped to listen for any sound of pursuit from the roof, the silence was deep enough to make the ears ring.

"I don't like this," Gil said. "We should hear the crew working down there. Maybe I should have called Max Goff first. . . ."

At the foot of the stairway they found the great central shaft lighted dimly by a single floodlamp, still and empty except for the *Phoebe I* and her unfinished sister.

"That isn't right," Gil said. "It isn't right at all."

Concern grew on his round face when the walls rattled his voice back at him. "I left Max in charge, with orders to keep the staff under cover. They should be here now."

They entered the workroom and angled past the silent ships toward the living quarters above. Halfway across the shaft the clang of a port swinging open halted them, the sound echoing in emptiness and drawing their attention sharply to the *Phoebe I*.

Max Goff stood in the open port, outlined in a flood of white light from the control room inside. He still wore his stained laboratory whites, and his red hair bristled wildly over his strained face. He held a shock-rod in his hand.

"Gil!" he called, and dropped down the short personnel ladder toward them. "Thank God you got here! I was afraid the patrols might have cut you off."

Gil met him halfway. "What's happened, Max? Where are the others?"

"I sent them away," Max said. "While there was time." He shook himself wearily. "Someone—Conniston's men, I think—got to Campion. He went out to see his family, and didn't come back. They're watching everyone, trying to get a line on you."

"Why Conniston? It could have been Solar or Government."

"Your escape from Ohio Peace Center was on the visi-news," Max said. "Conniston put out a special bulletin offering a reward for you—alive. He thinks he can still win with our help, and he wants you badly enough to draw off a large

115

part of his force to find you—his crews are combing the city, looking from house to house for the lab here. They may find it any minute."

"Then we'll have to run again," Gil said. His round shoulders slumped wearily.

"I waited in the *Phoebe*, hoping you'd make it in time," Max said. "We can go the way I'd planned to go, if you like —through the roof."

Gil nodded reluctantly. "We've no choice, it seems. We'd never stand trial now, no matter who finds us."

He turned toward the corridor that led to his office. "Get Miss Nugent and Paul aboard the *Phoebe*, Max. I'll be with you as soon as I pick up some records—the light-drive components are in my files, and I can't afford to leave them behind."

He hurried away. Max Goff turned eagerly to the ship, ushering Shannon and Ruth ahead. Shannon, at the ladder, stood fast.

"You should have a medical stock here," he said. "Can you give me a stimulant of some sort for Ruth? She's had a rough time for the past couple of days."

Goff hesitated. "In the first-aid room. Come this way."

They followed him to another corridor that paralleled the one Gil had taken. Ruth took Shannon's lead without questioning, but he caught her look and squeezed her arm warningly. At the corridor's end Goff switched on a light in the first-aid room and opened a white metal cabinet.

"Never mind the stimulant," Shannon said. "I see what I want."

He took the dart-gun out of his pocket and turned it on Goff. His tone warned the technician; Goff turned quickly, snatching at the shock-rod in his belt.

"Careful," Shannon warned. "Put the shock-rod on the table."

Goff stared at him, weighing the resolution in Shannon's face before he obeyed. Shannon took it up and beamed him out.

"He'll come round," he said, when Ruth cried out. "Goff is a part of this thing—can't you see that all this talk of

116

escape is only another trick to get us out of the way, to keep us quiet?"

He took a flat metal case from the medicine cabinet. Opened, it displayed a gleaming hypodermic needle and a neat row of ampules filled with a pale brownish liquid.

"*Hypnol!*" Ruth said. "You're planning to get the truth from Gil with *that.*"

"If it will work on a Cubist," Shannon said grimly. "And I think it will."

They found Gil in his office, stuffing papers into a brief case. He looked up sharply at their entrance, surprise in his eyes when he saw that Goff was not with them. "Where's Max?"

Shannon put the hypnol case on the desk. "In the first-aid room. He'll be out long enough for me to get the answers I want."

He winced a little when Gil recoiled from the case with its glittering contents. "I hate doing this, Gil, but I've no choice. You've put me off too long."

Gil wet his lips. "You're making a mistake, Paul. You'll be sorry if I tell you—it's not a thing you should know, either of you, and the knowledge won't help you if you get it. It's against the Plan—"

"I thought so," Shannon said. "I think I'd have guessed it long ago, if I hadn't let friendship blind me."

Every improbable incident in the plot that had brought him to this moment came back to him, falling into place with an inexorable clarity that left him shaken to the core with reaction. Against his will his whole existence had been ordered and altered, stripped of everything that had made it bearable; he had lost Ellen, and now Gil, and had nothing remaining but weary purpose.

"You were at the bottom of it all," Shannon said. "From the night I landed at the Garrick place you pulled the strings that led me on there and held me back here. I should have known it when the fat man—the Bearer—turned up at Peace Center.

"The suit and wallet and the rest of it had to be more of the same misdirection, because no one but you or Ellen would have known where to find them. You must even have

117

known where I was during those two years of hell I spent on Io, or you wouldn't have known when to expect me back. How, and why?"

Gil said soberly, "It does sound like a plot. Has it occurred to you that the whole thing might have been a psychological smoke screen thrown up to force you out on your own, to stretch you to your limits and see how you'd react? A trial to learn if the cutting edge of a new tool would be hard enough for the work laid out for it?"

They faced each other across the desk, Shannon tense and wary, Gil relaxed and patient. Ruth watched them uneasily from the corridor door, shivering in the draft from the cold hangar room.

Shannon called her to him and passed the shock-rod over.

"Hold him with this," he ordered. He took up the hypnol needle and charged it. "Don't make us beam you out, Gil. I'll only load you aboard the ship and give you the injection when you wake up. I'm through being driven like a sheep—I want the truth!"

Gil made a gesture of resignation.

"I can't afford the time it would take to come out of a hypnol trance—I'm going to be needed here. I'll tell you, if I must."

"So Goff's story *was* a red herring," Shannon said. "Conniston isn't as anxious as that to find you."

"Don't believe it," Gil warned. "Conniston is desperate for help, Paul—and so are Solar and the other syndicates and Government. This is open war, and the faction that wins—"

The floor underfoot heaved sharply and subsided to a faint, sustained trembling. Seconds later the dull rumble of an explosion rattled the hangar windows, a deep and ominous roar muffled by distance.

"They've begun it in earnest," Gil said. "That wasn't a detonite bomb, Paul. It was atomic."

He moved around the desk toward Shannon, a sudden shine of perspiration damping his forehead. "You've got to get out of here. If you won't think of yourself, for God's sake consider Ruth!"

Shannon shook his head. "Tell me what I want to know,
118

first. We'll run when I know what we're running from."

Gil drew back his desk chair and sat down. A suggestion of his old wry smile touched his face, showing the square edges of his widely spaced teeth.

"I helped make you what you are," he said. There was real affection in his voice. "I might have known you'd be hard enough to get what you want."

"Don't stall," Shannon said. "Get to it!"

"You didn't recognize the analogy I gave you on our way back from Peace Center, about the functioning of the sub-conscious and its control of systemic cell balance through hormones." He spoke rapidly now, like a man racing against time. "But consider this: when the body finds itself in imbalance from cellular disorder, it releases hormones designed to correct that disorder by setting up a new and stable balance. Would you say that the hormone itself is an intelligent factor in that correction, or a responsible agent? Does it know who, or what, sent it on its errand, or does the conscious mind of the body that secreted it know?"

They stared at him uncomprehendingly.

"The analogy isn't perfect," Gil said. "But it serves. The Cubes correspond roughly to hormones—they're corrective agents, insentient and without pity or malice. The entirety of intelligent life on all planets of the galaxy—in Earth's case, the human race—constitutes a cell in the being of a cosmic creature so large that it sprawls across a large part of the universe, an entity so vast that it is no more con-sciously aware of its own individual cells than we are aware of our own. But its subconscious knows.

"Technological factors during the past few centuries have raised human unrest on an exponential curve—the striving for existence between us has put every man literally at war with his own neighbor, and that warring amounts to the rebellious malfunctioning of a body-cell that refuses to work in normal harmony with others about it. Unchecked, the coming of stellar flight would have spread our unrest to other worlds and set up cells as wildly active as our own; the end result would have been the same to the galactic entity of which we are a part as cancer would be to us—an

119

uncontrollable malignancy that would eventually destroy its parent body.

"That is why the Cubes must win. They are thrown against us not with any malice but from necessity, cosmic antibodies bringing us stability, which is peace. The governing subconscious of the entity out there has finally sensed the danger we represent, and has taken steps to quiet us."

Another blast, closer this time, shook the warehouse. "That will be Boston Suburban," Gil said. "*Will* you go, Paul?"

When Shannon made no move to go he stood up, irony mingling with the urgency in his voice.

"Doesn't it stagger you that in spite of all our scheming and struggling, we've managed to become nothing better than a local irritant to a creature that doesn't even know we exist?"

CHAPTER EIGHTEEN

It was more than staggering.

"It's not even a plausible lie," Shannon said. He shut his mind against the stunning concept, penning it behind a wall of disbelief.

Gil said with a terrible earnestness, "It's no lie, Paul. Your own cells are active—how do you know they're not intelligent, too? How would an influx of hormones trying to restore balance seem to them—like champions, or like invaders?"

"It's against all reason," Shannon said stubbornly. "If that were true, the Bearer wouldn't have refused Ruth and me at Peace Center yesterday. Why should we be different?"

"Because you're cutting tools reserved for a particular purpose, and the time to use you hasn't come yet. There's a difference among Cubists, Paul: my kind, then the Bearers and the Servants, and then the rank and file. A society of sheep is stable but static—some of us must retain a modified initiative to keep the wheels of existence turning."

"And Ruth and I?"

"You're not affected. Healthy cells grow too, and multiply. You're being—transplanted."

The radophone on Gil's desk buzzed gently, the soft sound falling like a thunderclap between them. Ruth dropped her shock-rod without noticing, watching the screen with wide eyes.

"Don't answer it," Shannon said. "No one knows we're here—it may be a trap."

Gil pressed the activating stud. "But it may be one of my staff, needing help. I'll have to answer."

The radophone screen sprang to life. Zimmer Conniston looked out at them.

"Lucas!" he said hoarsely. "For God's sake, Lucas, come to me! I'm going to lose this fight without you!"

"You were lost from the beginning, Conniston," Gil said. "Haven't you learned that already?"

Two nights before, seeing Conniston on the radophone at Ansel's pledge-shop, Shannon had been struck with the uncertainty in his manner. Tonight the Guild leader's panic was too plain to mistake, warping his heavy-jowled face and rounding his eyes like a frightened child's.

"Don't argue," Conniston urged. "The civil patrols are searching everywhere for you. There's no time to waste!"

Gil said sharply, "How do you know that? Who told you where to find me?"

Conniston turned conciliatory. "Campion. But I didn't have time to use the information before Orsham picked up more of your staff and wrung them dry."

"Campion didn't tell you willingly," Gil said. Slow anger roughened his mild voice. "You forced it out of him, Conniston, but it won't help you. You're done for, because your muscle squads aren't equipped to fight Government and the syndicates both. They're caught in the middle like the public, and like the public they'll turn to the Cubes when the going gets rough. When it's all over, none of them will be left—not even you."

A third blast shook the warehouse to its foundations. The radophone screen swirled madly, rioting with flying spirals of color. When it steadied, Conniston's face had gone slack

121

with shock. An ugly bruise marked the Guild leader's cheek; his nose dripped blood, slowly.

"That was—close," he said thickly. "Solar—striking back. Or Government—"

He pulled himself together and turned his pleas to Shannon.

"You're a practical man, Shannon. Bring Lucas to me and I'll give you anything you want. I'll clear you with Government . . ."

Shannon cut him off in disgust. "Help you, after what you did to Ellen's mother? Conniston, you're a greater fool than I thought!"

"I had forgotten the girl," Conniston said.

His pale eyes lighted. "I'll bargain with you for Lucas, then. My men brought your fiancee back from Peace Center before you were well out of Metro. She's been here since —bring Lucas to me, and I'll give her back to you."

To Shannon it was like having the floor drawn suddenly from beneath his feet. If they had Ellen there—

He saw the unlikeliness of it even before Gil warned, "Don't be a fool, Paul. He's lying."

"Of course," Shannon said. And to Conniston: "You'd have no reason to keep Ellen there, even if you had her, once Gil and I were arrested at Peace Center. You'd have released or killed her by now."

In his frustration, Conniston lost all control. "I tell you she's here, Shannon! Not in my office, but in the building. I'll send for her!"

"You'll send a squad of musclers instead," Shannon said. He turned his back on the screen. "Let's go, Gil. I'm not through with you yet."

Ruth said worriedly, "Can't we use the *Phoebe* to go to my father? He'll be frantic about me, and we'll be safer out there on—"

Shannon put a rough hand over her mouth, silencing her.

"Orsham's crew is already looking for the *Ark*," he said in her ear. "Will you put Conniston after her, too?"

He felt the sudden fall of silence behind them and turned to see the Guild leader staring after them from the rado-phone screen, his face a study in startled comprehension.

"Conniston heard what you said," Shannon grumbled when they were in the corridor. "And he'll probably make the most of it. He'll have every patrol craft in the system alerted for us before we're out of atmosphere."

Ruth answered him with a defiant tilt of her head, but the brightness of her eyes gave her away. To Shannon the realization that she must be very near the breaking-point came as a minor shock; it had never occurred to him, caught up in the headlong confusion of his search, that there might be a limit to her stamina.

"I doubt that it'll matter," he said, trying to reassure her. "Conniston should have his hands too full here to chase after us."

"He can try," Gil said. "But no ordinary craft will ever overhaul the *Phoebe*."

He paused at the corridor mouth to look with pride in his eyes at the sleek vertical bulk of the little ship in the hangar. "She's adapted to use your father's light-drive, Ruth. Nothing short of the *Ark* herself will overtake her."

"The light-drive?" Ruth said, incredulously. "How did you get hold of *that*?"

Gil gave her a smile edged with faint malice. "Through one of your father's trusted staff. There are more of us than you might—"

A heavy blast just outside the warehouse cut him short.

The workroom floor shuddered under their feet; dust from the concussion, shaken from the roof overhead, settled about them in gray, tenuous plumes. The roar of sound had not died away when a sharper explosion on the roof above sent a gust of smoke billowing into the hangar from the stairwell entrance.

"The civil patrols," Gil said. "Or Solar's muscle squads—Conniston wasn't lying about them after all!"

They ran for the ship, the scuffing of their feet on the concrete drowned in the heavier sound of men rushing down the staircase.

They reached the personnel ladder at the *Phoebe*'s open port before pursuit appeared. Shannon boosted Ruth inside and put down a hand to Gil, who had stopped short at the bottom rung.

123

"I'm not going," Gil said. He stepped back from Shannon's outstretched hand. "I'm sorry, Paul. I'd hoped the break wouldn't come so soon, but I'm needed here. There's no place in the Plan for me on Io."

Shannon swore bitterly and turned the dart-gun on him. From behind, Ruth's hands pulled at him urgently. "Hurry, Paul! Oh, why don't you let him go before it's too late!"

Shannon shook her off. "Climb up, Gil. Don't make me come after you!"

A civil patrolman in dusty green uniform appeared on the stairway, others crowding behind him. Metal glinted; something whispered past Shannon's face and exploded deafeningly against the farther wall of the hangar.

He fired back automatically, and felt his stomach lurch sickly when the man disappeared in a gout of smoke and red flame. In the crackling tunnel of the stairwell someone else screamed piercingly.

Gil stood fast, a shadow of familiar Cubist serenity touching his round, earnest face.

"It's no good, Paul," he said. "You couldn't change Ellen back to Normal when you found her. You couldn't change me, either. I told you the truth about the Cubes back there in the office. I'd have spared you the knowing if I could, but you'll never see either of us again."

He turned and went toward the first-aid room where Max Goff still lay unconscious.

Shannon set a foot on the personnel ladder to go after him, and drew it back when a shattering detonation outside smashed a gaping breach in the hangar's southern wall. Through the swirl of dust and smoke he glimpsed running figures pouring in through the break, and behind them others swarming up from the street.

He stepped back into the ship and slammed the port. Air hissed behind him, sealing the lock. At the control panel Ruth was belting herself into the massive pilot's chair, her eyes scanning the relay studs as she worked.

"Strap yourself into the other seat," she called. "Hurry—we're taking off!"

Shannon stood panting in the center of the room, dazed past understanding her by his confusion of anger and frus-

124

tration. The sudden overwhelming weight of acceleration drove him to the floor, smashed the breath out of his lungs and struck a leaden paralysis through his body.

There was a rending clangor of tearing metal as the *Phoebe* ripped through the hangar roof. The sound echoed deafeningly back and forth inside the ship, and with its dying away the intolerable pressure left Shannon as suddenly as it had come.

He drifted up slowly from near unconsciousness, not caring, for the moment, whether or not he was injured. When he sat up to orient himself, he found that Ruth had unstrapped herself and was watching him curiously from the control board.

"We're out of atmosphere," she said. "And ready to use the light-drive. If it follows the *Ark's* principle as closely as I think it does, we'll be on Io in less than an hour."

Shannon, making no effort to move while his bruised body gathered strength to stand, thought wearily that with her taking command of the *Phoebe* Ruth had turned the tables on him completely. She had put on her old assurance like a familiar garment, and reverted on the instant to the self-sufficient capability he had first known. Given her brown coveralls instead of the stained and disheveled party dress, she would have looked exactly as she had looked when he saw her first.

"And getting to the *Ark* will put the Plan on schedule again, I suppose," he said bitterly. "I'm still in good hands. . . . The Plan takes a change of worlds in its stride—why shouldn't it include a change of guardians?"

She left the control chair and came toward him, her eyes angry. Shannon got up with an effort that left him trembling and faced her.

"I never supposed you really thought I was a Cubist," Ruth said. "Would I have—oh, why do I waste time trying to convince you? What difference can it possibly make whether you believe me or not?"

"None whatever," Shannon said. Defeat rode him, weighing him down with a sense of futility greater than he could bear. "The Plan will be served, it seems, and nothing else matters."

125

An Earth Gone Mad

With dull irrelevance he recalled a fanciful old account he had once read at school concerning a man who had no country, an outcast condemned all his life to sail the seas without setting foot on land. That one, Shannon thought, had suffered nothing by comparison; he, Shannon, had lost not only his country but his world as well, his fiancee, his friend and at the same time all sense of belonging to his own species.

Even on Io he had never known what being truly alone could be like; there had been the Kyril for companionship then, and the anticipation of returning home, to bolster him against despair. Now there was nothing left but an appalling emptiness and the dreary prospect of being shoved about again like a chess pawn in an endless game played by an invisible but monstrously capable opponent.

"Will you open the shutters?" he asked. He remembered how Earth had looked when he came down from Io—green-brown and smiling, adance with water-glints through veils of sun-soft clouds—and felt a masochistic desire to relive the moment. "I'd like to see Earth again."

Ruth went back to the control panel and touched a stud that rolled the port shutters back like spools of jointed metal tape into the walls, and he could see Earth.

The *Phoebe* lay squarely in the dull red cone of the planetary penumbra, cut off from sight of the Sun by Earth's vast, dark bulk. To one side of the ship hung a thin, stark crescent of Moon; on the other, the tiny red and silver disks of Mars and Jupiter. Beyond them lay the vast yawning pit of space, utter blackness spangled and glittering with myriad drifts of stars.

Looking down the cone of the penumbra was like sighting along a monstrous tunnel that dwindled in sharp perspective, a cosmic bore dim with blood-hued shadow and truncated abruptly at Earth's night-side hemisphere, a titanic black disk edged with a sullen furnace-glow of air-diffracted sunlight. To Shannon, Earth looked like a world on fire; and it came to him, with a flash of new-found perception, that the thought was no sort of hysteric symbolism but a literal awareness of global holocaust. Earth *was* on fire, burning as

126

she had burned for millennia with the senseless perpetual warrings of her children.

But burning brighter now, like a faggot on blown coals.

Until now the fire had smoldered, never going out but building slowly. And in its present final fury it was accomplishing nothing more than the summoning of alien monitors from *out there* to extinguish its burning—and freedom with it.

The thought brought a sharp recurrence of the shock he had felt, and suppressed, when Gil Lucas had told him what lay behind the Cubes. For the moment he could see Gil's face limned against the conflagration, round and harassed and reluctant, and hear the deadly seriousness of his voice detailing the terrible simplicity of the Plan.

For the first time belief came to Shannon, and the reality of it was more chilling in the black detachment of space than it could ever have been on Earth. Horror shook him like a plunge into icy water; when he turned from the port he was sweating and his hands shook uncontrollably.

"What if Gil was right?" he asked. "What if the sort of cosmic brute he described really *is* hovering out there somewhere, using us but too monstrously big to be conscious of us?"

When she answered, he saw that she had accepted the premise already and had adapted herself as to a reality. Her composure surprised and shamed him.

"And suppose there is?" she said calmly. "If Gil was right, it's been there forever, and never threatened us until we forced it to. Gil called our trouble a moral anarchy, once, but we don't have to make the same mistake again. With a stable nucleus like the *Ark*'s crew, we can start over and do a better job of bringing up a race than we did before. What is happening down there now needn't be the end, but only a step toward a better beginning."

Surprisingly, her calm acceptance was as soothing as a sedative.

Understanding of his own panic came like a corollary to her logic. His fear had not been altogether for his own life; it was the individual's instinctive terror at the prospect of complete and final racial death. For a man to die among his

127

friends, he thought, is a terrifying but commonplace thing; but for the last man alive—knowing that after him there could be no others, that the perpetuity of which he had been a part was about to cease forever—it could be infinitely more awful.

Yet if that last man were represented by a picked group like Nugent's crew, escaping that finality to transplant humanity to the stars, carrying with them the phoenix of immortality . . .

"I believe you're right," Shannon said.

He thought of the virgin worlds lying empty and waiting, system after system swinging within reach of Nugent's light-drive, and the challenge of their strangeness and promise touched his imagination with a quick stir of interest.

"You've *got* to be right," he said. "And if you are, we're wasting time. Let's go on to the *Ark*."

She made room for him at the instrument panel, and they sat together in the twin chairs at the controls.

"We'll have to take a bearing first," Ruth said. Her fingers moved over the computer studs, feeding data into the calculator banks while she talked. "With the light-drive, we don't have to bother with orbital figures and escape speeds. Planetary ellipses are too small in arc to matter, and we've only to consider galactic spin and the tangenital drift of the Sun. Gravitic strains are everywhere, no matter—"

"I've heard the principle explained before," Shannon said. "But I didn't understand it then, and shouldn't understand it any better now. You're out of my depth before you start."

She laughed at his admission, and sobered quickly. "You've heard it before? From whom?"

"From Max Goff," Shannon said.

For a moment he could see Max's face again, stereo-sharp in memory, animated and eager as he tried to explain in layman's terms a concept that could not be expressed except in mathematical symbols. At this instant Goff might be lying on the floor of the first-aid room, still gripped in shock-ray paralysis, unless Gil had roused him in time. Or unless another bomb had leveled the warehouse on them all, or the inrushing patrols had . . .

"Poor Max," he said. "And Gil—my God, *Gil!* Why did

128

things have to go like this?"

She put a hand on his arm, sensing his torment and react-
ing with quick sympathy. "Don't blame yourself, Paul. What
happened back there was only a part of what had to happen
—Gil understood that, and wanted to spare you the pain of
knowing it."

"I know," Shannon said. "He'd have kept it from me, if
I had let him. . .   Ruth, Gil must have stood high in the
Cubist Plan to have arranged things as he did, had you
thought of that? And his whole function, since he never
really worked with Conniston against the Cubes, must have
been to guide you and me through the confusion and get us
safely out of it. But why? Why should our escaping be so
important?"

She gave him a look of mingled amusement and annoyance.

"I believe you really don't know. But I shouldn't worry
about it, if I were you. The Bearer promised you'd know
everything in due time, and I think you will."

He pressed her for an explanation, and she turned back
to the controls to evade it.

"We're going on light-drive," she said. She drew an improbably traced tape from the bearing calculator and fed it
into another mechanism as incomprehensible to Shannon.
"Look outside."

CHAPTER NINETEEN

HE STOOD in awe at the port, shaken and at the same time
exhilarated by the strangeness that had fallen upon the
familiar space beyond the glass.

Space was no longer black. A faint pearly sheen glowed
through it, shot with a million million starpoints familiar
enough in placement but blazing in crescendo up the spec-
trum like a shower of sparks from a brazer's wheel. Yellow
stars changed to white while he watched; the white turned
blue and then violet, and vanished.

The glare of sunlight through the port dulled to a sullen,
brooding red. Shannon, startled, found himself able to stare

directly at the Sun without discomfort, a fading and ominous coin-sized disk set against a blackness deeper than his perception could grasp.

"It looks like a dying coal," he breathed. "Like a cinder out of hell!"

Ruth came to stand beside him, as pleased over the display as another woman might have been pleased at showing off a new gown.

"Doppler effect," she said. "You've known about it all your life—it's been used to measure the spectral drift of starlight for hundreds of years. But it *is* strange to be able to see it, isn't it?"

Shannon let out his breath raggedly. "It's pretty terrifying. What would happen if we struck a meteor at this speed? A fission blast?"

"You've touched on the point that makes the light-drive practical," Ruth said. "The ship's distortion-bubble goes ahead of us, as it must if the space-strain behind it is to move us on. Any mass caught in the advance field loses all gravitic weight, keeping only inertia; it never actually reaches the ship, but is carried before it. When we break out of light-drive, the accumulated matter we've picked up comes out with us at the same rate of speed, so that its mass isn't dangerous at all. We've only to move through or around it."

She looked thoughtful. "Father and Alec say that the *Ark* might even drive through the heart of a planet without being damaged. I hope they're right!"

They stood at the port together until a signal chimed at the instrument board and Ruth ran back to her controls. There was no sense of strain, nor of deceleration, but the violet points of stars that broke through the haze ahead began to shift swiftly down the scale to normal color. Sunlight returned, bright and yellow, but noticeably weaker than before.

"We're coming out," Ruth said. A brief puff of dust swirled past the ports and was gone, glittering like powdered mica in the sunlight. "A meteor, or what's left of it. We're inside Ganymede's orbit already   . there's Io!"

Jupiter dominated the sky like a monstrous silver ball,

flattened and tarnished and banded with murky striae, the great oval of the Red Spot glaring out at its satellite system like a jealous, angry eye. Shannon, searching past the wheeling straw-colored crescent of Io, picked out Callisto's steelgray disk swinging in toward eclipse behind the parent planet's bulk.

"I was bound there when the *Flora* went out of control and crashed on Io," he said. "I wonder what things would be like now if I had made that trip safely? If I hadn't lost those two years, Ellen and I might have—"

Ruth interrupted without seeming to hear him. "You'd better strap yourself in. I'm cutting in the atomics for landing."

They settled toward a bleak landscape as familiar to Shannon as the back of his hand, a cruel and pitiless place of jagged obsidian mountains and green jungles spotted with blatant flame-vines flowers glowing a sullen, venous red. There was no sign of the *Ark*, nor of any human occupation.

Shannon was about to protest that no ship of the *Ark's* size could be hidden on Io when Ruth grounded the *Phoebe* at the base of a towering basalt mesa. He saw then that the mesa was not a true tableland but two peaks split by a deep ravine; from either side of the cleft a cunningly latticed screen had been swung, camouflaged so that its upper side blended perfectly with the twisting Ionian terrain.

On the canyon floor beneath lay the *Ark*, ports open, armed men scurrying in tight knots about her to outlying gun emplacements. Shannon caught a glimpse of Alec Blair's slight figure, bare sandy hair glinting in the pale sunlight. Dace Nugent appeared in the *Ark's* rearmost port, the stubby bulk of an exploder cradled in his arms.

The camouflage was clever enough, but Nugent's allowing an unidentified ship to land within a hundred yards of his own was proof enough that the *Ark* was equipped with nothing in the way of offensive weapons. They had stocked nothing, apparently, but light weapons; the *Ark*, Shannon thought derisively, would be a sitting duck for the smallest patrol boat equipped with a missile-launcher.

He had expected Ruth to run out at once when he opened the *Phoebe's* port, and was surprised when she hesitated in the opening. Even when the *Ark's* crew recognized her and came running across the rocky distance to meet her she showed no eagerness. Instead she turned a troubled face to Shannon, more uncertain now than he had seen her since they first met.

"Please don't be bitter about what you've lost," she said. "You did all that could be done, Paul, more than anyone I've ever known could have done." And, before he could answer: "I'm glad you're coming with us to Procyon. I never thought I'd be glad, but I am."

He searched for the irony he suspected, and was surprised to find none.

"What else can I do?" he said. "There's nowhere else to go, now."

She bit her lip and turned to the port ladder. Shannon followed her down, scowling, disturbed by an unaccountable sense of having bungled an overture.

Dace Nugent met them, his lined face alight with relief. He caught his daughter to him, found the exploder an encumbrance and flung it away. The two of them stood together wordlessly until Shannon shifted restively. The *Ark's* crew streamed toward them from makeshift gun emplacements, cheering.

"You came just in time," Nugent said huskily. "I've gone half mad here, trying to work out a way to find you without giving the *Ark* away. Another day, and we'd have had to blast off without you."

"Paul brought me back," she said. She drew back from her father, her eyes shining. "We took the long way round, but we're here."

Nugent held out his hand to Shannon, and drew it back blankly when Shannon ignored it.

"You'd really have gone without her," Shannon said incredulously. "You'd have left her back there, knowing what's going on!"

Ruth laughed, a clear peal of sound utterly out of place in the harsh Ionian stillness.

"Father is a *practical* idealist, Paul," she said. "All of us are, or we'd never have been chosen for this flight in the beginning. The project is more important than any of us."

An Earth Gone Mad

When Shannon said nothing, she added pointedly: "You were on the point of deserting me yourself once, if you'll remember. Why didn't you?"

"I don't know," Shannon said. And, in sudden honesty: "But I'm glad I didn't. Neither of us would be here now if I had."

The Nugents smiled together. The *Ark's* crew surrounded them, congratulating Ruth, shaking Shannon's hand against his will.

Alec Blair came up, panting, and Nugent turned on him without giving him time to greet Ruth. "We're ready to blast off as soon as you can give us a course," Nugent said. "How long will you need?"

"Four hours, minimum," Blair said tersely. "I'll put the astrogation team on it right away."

He ignored Shannon and held out both hands to Ruth. "Welcome home, darling. . . ."

Later, Shannon let Ruth and Dace Nugent lead him through the *Ark* from cargo holds to navigation room, listening with bleak disinterest to Nugent's explanation of the ship's appointments. At another time his engineer's sense of thoroughness would have been delighted, but at the moment his growing conviction of irremediable loss was too crushing to leave room for appreciation.

He met the *Ark's* crew, by sections, and was forced to admit that Nugent had proved himself a shrewd judge of character and ability. The ship was manned by an eminently capable staff, a cheerful but resolute group who could clearly be depended on to live together sensibly and without friction. Most were technicians of one sort or another, and so not likely to make the hardiest of pioneers, but they were stable beyond argument.

They were in the green room when Ruth saw herself in the glass panes of an algae tank and cried out in dismay.

"I'm going to hide until I get rid of my dirt and rags," she said, ruefully. "I'll be around again before blastoff time, if I can make it."

But at the exit she hesitated to look over the close-packed beds of healthy greenery. "All the comforts of home," she said. "Fresh air and vegetables and a complete stock of ani-

133

mals for the new world. . . . It won't be like Earth for a while, wherever it is, but we'll make it do."

They left the green room and went with her as far as the metabolic suspension chamber, a place tiered with coffin-sized chests recessed like vaults into the walls. Nugent opened one and slid out a hermetically sealed plastiglass box, padded throughout with foam rubber and equipped with a self-contained air purifier.

"One of the penalties of protracted flight," he said. "But the length of the trip makes it unavoidable. Many of us are no longer young—competent specialists seldom are—and twelve years would see us too old to be useful when we reach the new world. To compensate for that we've provided suspension chambers for the older members and for sick and injured whose treatment may take considerable time."

Idly Shannon counted the vaults, and found their number surprisingly small.

"Fifty-eight," he said. "Your number must be twice that. Why not a cell for each member except the flight crew?"

Nugent laughed. "There was some discussion on that point, but since the aim of any colonizing expedition is to populate new worlds as quickly as possible we elected to leave the younger members active during the trip. There are one hundred eight of us, twenty-seven men and eighty-one women, of whom fifty-eight will sleep through the trip unless emergency forces us to wake them. The others will be busy maintaining ship's operation and bringing up the new generation."

"New generation?" Understanding came, and with it an increased respect for Nugent's thoroughness. "I see. By the time you reach Procyon there should be children old enough to lend a hand with the colonizing."

"We've provided nurseries and schooling facilities," Nugent said. "With special emphasis on the schooling. There is no human failing—and this includes man's natural belliger-ence, Shannon—that cannot be tempered by proper condi-tioning. Those children will have a better chance to grow into really stable adults than any single group ever born."

"It sounds practical enough," Shannon said.

A memory from his copter flight with Ruth to Peace Center came back to amuse him briefly. "Will your marital groups be selected according to eugenic fitness, special abilities, or by choice?"

"By choice, of course," Ruth said. She flushed at his sardonic look, and he saw that she remembered the incident as well. "But one thing is certain, Paul Shannon—there'll be no *bargains* driven in the selecting!"

She left them then and went on to the forward part of the ship. Shannon and Nugent, following more slowly, found the astrogation room a place of quiet activity, a five-man team of flight technicians working busily at a bank of computing machines to plot the *Ark's* course.

Alec Blair was in charge, too engrossed in his work to spare more than a nod to Nugent and an indifferent glance at Shannon. Nugent, reluctant to interrupt the work by lingering, led the way forward again, and they ended the tour in the shuttered observation chamber at the *Ark's* bow.

Shannon drew the shutters and stood in half-listening attention to Nugent's monologue while he stared out over the bleak Ionian badlands. At the moment, he was not thinking of the holocaust behind nor of the flight ahead, but of the two years he had spent here. By comparison with what he had recently gone through, he found those hard-lived months almost attractive, and for the dozenth time the Kyril's cryptic prophecy came to mind: ". . . *lost touch with your own world. You may wish, later* . ."

He realized then that the Kyril had been right, and on the heels of the understanding came a nostalgic desire that surprised him because he had not thought it possible. It would be good to see the Kyril again, to assure himself that he still had one friend in a universe of strangers.

As if in answer to the thought he glimpsed a vague suggestion of disharmony in the harsh angularity of the ravine beyond the *Ark*, a hint of even curvature that jarred against the jagged patterns of unweathered stone. It was either an improbably rounded boulder, he thought, or—the possibility brought a slight lift of excitement—it was the Kyril.

"I'm going out," he said abruptly, and opened the bow port. Nugent stared after him blankly, and Shannon shrugged off his unspoken question.

"Be careful," Nugent warned. "It's getting late, and the lava-lions will be out."

"I know them," Shannon said. "I'll be back by blastoff time. If I'm not, leave me. It won't make a great deal of difference."

He went down the ravine with a growing sense of anticipation, as if he were on his way to keep an appointment with an old and valued friend. His uncertainty was settled within a matter of minutes.

The Kyril was waiting for him.

"You are late, Paul Shannon," the Kyril said. Its telepathic voice was as coolly unhurried as ever; the familiar feel of it left Shannon with a curious sense of comfort, as if he had just waked to find his late ordeal an inconsequential dream. "I had begun to think I should have to call you."

Shannon, assuming unconsciously a position he had used a thousand times before with his enigmatic friend, sat on his haunches and looked curiously up at the Kyril's lichened shape.

"You told me when I left Io that I had changed," he said, "and that I might wish later that I had stayed here. Did you know then what was happening on Earth, Kyril? Do you know what has happened since?"

"I knew," the Kyril said. "But I could not tell you. You were not ready to know. It was necessary that you solve the problems forced upon you or that you fall before them."

Shannon stood up, startled by the inference. "You knew? Then you must be—"

He drew back, chilled, understanding what he had only guessed vaguely at before. "Kyril, you're a prime mover in this madman's dream! You fit into it somehow, just as Gil did!"

"Your friend would have spared you knowing all this," the Kyril said. "But you were determined, and difficult. Are you any the happier now for understanding?"

Shannon was torn by a confusion of emotions: anger at the Kyril for the deception, resentment tempered by a chill of uneasiness at the thought of having lived for two years with one of the alien things that had brought all this about.

"It's hard to believe," he said slowly. "And yet—"

136

An Earth Gone Mad

"Yet it is true," the Kyril said. "And inevitable. To exist, any organism must maintain peace and harmony within its being, or die. To continue in existence, it must grow; cells dying or killed must be replaced, and others added. Your Earth cell, so far as growth is concerned, is not dead but static—you and these others with you must replace it elsewhere."

"So that's it," Shannon said. "The purpose behind it all. The Plan."

The gigantic simplicity of it numbed him.

"And I fought against *this*," he said, remembering his early anger and his furious pygmy strugglings. "I was going to stop it all, to turn back everything as it was!"

"What happens on Earth does not happen often," the Kyril said, keeping pace with Shannon's thought. "Man is an exceptional case, one of the few species too aggressive to achieve balance alone. If he had been more rational and less greedy, this would never have come about."

The silent voice went on. "Stellar flight would have come to men in time, when they were ready for it, to insure their natural growth. You have been taught in a hard school that self-preservation is the strongest law of life—it is not. The will to grow, and through growth to extend the prime entity, is the law. Your adventurers in all times have proved it, venturing in flimsy boats across uncharted seas, facing dreadful individual deaths because in them was planted the instinct to spread sentient life across first a continent, then a globe, and after that to the stars. But such instruments as are used to spread that sentience must be at peace with themselves, else the growth will be warped. Do you follow me, Paul Shannon?"

It was impossible not to follow.

"A new cell arises from a fresh nucleus, and the whole will fail if that nucleus should prove too weak to survive the trials of growth. To prosper, it must be tempered and conditioned like a tool in a forge to serve its purpose.

"You, and these others, are such tools, untainted in any way with Cubist compulsion but nevertheless tempered for your parts. You will work together in the new world to establish the stable culture that should have been Earth's in the

137

beginning, and where the old failed, the new will succeed. Does that satisfy your need to know? And are you strong enough, now that you have it, to bear the knowledge?"

He was, and knew it, and did not say as much because the Kyril had known it first.

"Still you wonder about my place in the scheme," the Kyril said. "I am a local antibody, necessary but individually of no importance to the total organism. The Cubes are my instruments; they obey my direction, and with their success my function is done. There will be none of us in the worlds ahead of you, for there is no need of us there. The worlds you will reach may be peopled by hostile forms completely alien and unpleasant, or they may be beautiful beyond your imagination, lying fallow and waiting for your feet to make them yours. That is for you to learn."

A picture came to Shannon of the dark, endless depth of space, studded with suns flaming orange and blue and white and red; of circling green worlds and dead worlds of water and darkness and others of wind and sand and fire, and the terrible beauty of it exhilarated and awed him beyond his ability to endure. He suffered a brief dizziness that sprang from his effort to contain the intolerable understanding that had been given him.

When his vision cleared, the Kyril was gone.

CHAPTER TWENTY

THE SOUND of footsteps roused him with a start.

The Sun had gone down while he talked to the Kyril, and with the fall of evening Jupiter rose in a second dawn of cold silver light that made Io's desolation over into a fantastic fairyland. By the pale flood of light Shannon saw that it was not a lava-lion that came, but Ruth Nugent.

She had not gone back to her brown coveralls after all. Instead she had changed from the grimy party dress to another whose color Shannon could not make out in the hueless planet-glow, but which gave her a warm and unanswer-

able femininity that not even the chill efficiency of the exploder under her arm could lessen.

"I was afraid the lava-lions had caught you," she said. "I
came to take you back to the *Ark*. We blast off in less than
an hour."

He went toward her, astonished by the warmth of feeling
that surged up in him.

"I talked with the Kyril," he said. "I learned that what
Gil told us was true. I learned something else, too."

When she stood up quietly, he went on: "I asked myself
what sort of choice I might make if I could go back two
years from this moment and start over, and I discovered
that I didn't want my old life back. When I think of Earth,
I think of that poor stupid little Titanian at Ansel's place,
dying on its feet of its own appetites while it aped a thing
no better than itself. I'm starting over, Ruth, and for the
first time in my life, I'm at peace with myself. I'm looking
forward to that flight to Procyon."

She said in a small, careful voice: "And Ellen? You're
giving her up along with Earth?"

He made a futile, wordless sound. "I know how this will
sound, but I can't help it. I think I've changed even more
than Ellen—we couldn't be happy together now even if she
were not a Cubist. I've outgrown my old life—I think we've
all outgrown it, else we wouldn't be out here now, reaching
for the stars."

She sighed. "I know. I've changed too, since that flight to
Peace Center, more than I ever imagined I could change.
If I hadn't, I couldn't have made myself break with Alec
this evening."

He took a step nearer, trying to see what was in her eyes.
"You broke with Alec? Why?"

"For the same reason you gave up Ellen," she said serenely. "Because Alec is considerate and good and a very
brilliant physicist, but he's also a dry little man who could
never give me what I've had for the past few days—strength
and confidence, a sense of being needed and the certainty
of never being alone or afraid any more."

He said wonderingly, "But that's the way *I* feel, though
I couldn't have put it like that. I think that's when I first

realized that I had outgrown the old life, when I understood that none of this would have any meaning for me without you."

They stood for a moment with the planet-shine bright between them, shaken by the discovered bond between them.

"I've a one-track mind," Shannon said almost humbly, "and there wasn't room in it for both of us when we made that flight to Peace Center. But I'll have twelve years to make it up to you, Ruth."

She took the step that remained between them.

"More than that," she said. Her mouth had gone heavy and soft, and the warmth and tender strength of her recalled vividly the night she had comforted him on the Metro pier. "Much more than twelve years, Paul. And you won't have to bargain for me, now or ever."

Later, Shannon said, "I understand now why it was so important that Gil get us away from Earth. And I tried so hard to stop him!"

It was almost time for the blastoff when they reached the ship. Dace Nugent met them at the *Ark's* bow port, his square face lined with worry.

"I was about to start a search for you," he said. "There's a ship less than a hundred miles out, and I think it's searching for the *Ark*. We'll have to hurry."

Shannon was helping him to make the port fast when Alec Blair called urgently down the corridor, halting them.

Blair was panting when he reached them, his mild eyes hard with inner tension. "Leave it open," he said. "I'm going out and trigger the *Phoebe's* atomics for delayed fission. We can't have that light-drive of hers falling into the wrong hands—we'd have this hell to go through again some day. . . . The astrogators are asking for you in the control room, Dace."

Nugent left hurriedly, taking Ruth with him. When they had gone, Blair put out an unexpected hand to Shannon.

"Ruth put me straight this evening," he said. "I wish you both luck. I won't say I'm happy about it of course, but getting the *Ark* to Procyon is the important thing."

He went down the personnel ladder into the Jupiter-bright evening, running swiftly toward the upright copper shape of the *Phoebe*. Shannon, a little disconcerted, went back through the ship to the control room.

He found the astrogation team grouped tautly about the master visiscreen, their plotting forgotten.

"They've found us, Paul," Ruth said when he came in. She went directly to him, her eyes bright with tears. "To be so close, darling, and then to be dragged back to that—they *can't* stop us now! It wasn't meant to end like this!"

From the screen a young man in patrol captain's uniform looked out at them, his face tight and determined.

"I have orders from Government, on request of a patron, to hold you," he said. "Please don't try a surprise lift. We have an atomic seeker-missile directly over your ship and triggered to your mass—you'd be blasted to bits before you could begin accelation."

He turned his head briefly. "Cut in the beam relay. Put the patron on the circuit."

Zimmer Conniston's face replaced the patrol captain's, his familiar scowl blurred by the distortion of relay. He singled out Dace Nugent at once, ignoring the others.

"Don't risk a takeoff," he said urgently. "I don't want the *Ark* damaged. My staff and I are going with you, Nugent. There's nothing much of the Guild left, nor of Solar Government won't stand another week—"

"I won't take you!" Nugent said. "I'll wreck the ship first, Conniston! We're a picked crew—having your kind along would defeat our whole purpose. We'd only be starting over again with the same insanity we had before."

Conniston, characteristically, shifted his argument to Shannon. "Then it's up to you to hold them there until I come, Shannon. I've brought up an inducement to make it worth your while."

He turned his head. "Put the girl on the screen."

Someone shoved Ellen Keyne into view.

She took Shannon's stricken look calmly, wearing her serenity like a mantle. She remained on the screen for only a moment and was drawn away again.

"You'll get her back if you keep Nugent from ruining the
141

ship," Conniston said. "It's your choice, Shannon. All of us go to Procyon, or none."

His scowl lightened at the agony of indecision on Shannon's face. "Have all the ports opened to make sure they don't try to lift while the patrol crew takes over. My own ship is just outside the Martian ellipse—I'll be there in another six hours."

He waited, his scowl only half masking his anxiety, while Shannon made his choice.

Shannon took the dart-gun out of his pocket and turned it on Dace Nugent. "Send men to open the ports," he ordered. "Do as he says—*hurry!*"

Shannon went himself to the stern port, running through the *Ark's* echoing corridors with the bitter memory of Ruth's stricken, incredulous face before him. She had not cried out or pleaded against his decision, and her stunned acceptance tore him worse than any reproach she might have made.

He was halfway down the personnel ladder when the clanging of other ports sounded up and down the *Ark's* length. The vertical bullet-shape of the *Phoebe* stood outside, highlighted in the planet-shine, where he and Ruth had left it.

He remembered then that Blair had gone out to tamper with the little ship's safety controls, and prayed that the *Phoebe* might not be crippled beyond flight already.

Ruth's voice overtook him halfway to the *Phoebe*. "Paul, come back! I know what you're doing, but it isn't worth it! Paul, *please!*"

He looked back to see her on the port ladder, her eyes enormous with shock in the strained oval of her face. A cold fury of frustration seized him, shaking his resolution.

He could visualize exactly how it would be: the *Phoebe's* tiny shape rising like a bullet from beyond the seeker-missile's focus, flashing up on the new warping drive at near light-speed. The collision with the hovering guard ship at a velocity too great for comprehension, the nova-flash of atomic fission when the engine piles let go, the robot missile wandering away out of control, no longer a threat to the *Ark*—

If he had the courage to go through with it.

An Earth Gone Mad

"I've *got* to do it, Ruth," he cried up to her. "If I hadn't interfered, all of you would have been gone long ago. I'm not trying to be a damned stupid martyr—but the *Ark* is more important than any of us, don't you see?"

She called after him again. "Ellen is on Conniston's ship, Paul. Will you leave her to them?"

He did not stop. *Ellen is a Cubist,* he told himself. *What is death to her?*

"Then I'm coming with you!" Ruth cried.

He broke into a run to outdistance her—and was flung back, deafened and half stunned, when the *Phoebe* roared up and out of sight on a shattering blast of riven air.

Simultaneously, the blinding glare of collision in space touched him with a wave of heat like the opening of a furnace door.

When he could see again Ruth was kneeling beside him, crying softly.

"Poor Alec! He saw what was happening, working out there . . knew the chance you meant to take . . ."

"I know," Shannon said. He sat up, listening dully to the clanging of ports being closed up and down the *Ark*'s length. "He wasn't such a dry little man, after all. He was—"

From the port overhead someone called urgently: "Blast-off! Hurry, or they'll have to rechart the course!"

In the crew room they lay side by side on their padded acceleration couches, listening to the excited hum of voices rising from others strapped down like themselves against the *Ark*'s blastoff. At the last moment, Shannon put out a hand to Ruth across the little space between them. She took it and smiled without fear or uncertainty.

"The world is starting over again," she said. "And we're starting over with it. Paul, are you sorry?"

"I'll never be sorry," Shannon said. And added, out of the bitter memory of pain left behind: "We'll do a better job of it, this time. The star dice will never roll for us out there."

He thought of the picture the Kyril had shown him, of the endless velvet reaches of space ahead with their shining colored suns and cryptic, beckoning worlds.

"They'll wait," he said, irrelevantly. "They've waited for a million million years. Another twelve won't matter!"

They were still holding hands and laughing together when the *Ark* rushed up into the sky, toward the stars.

www.ingramcontent.com/pod-product-compliance
Lightning Source LLC
Chambersburg PA
CBHW021112130626
46554CB00002B/648